Disaster Du Jour

Stone Soup For Survival

Ron Foster

AlabamaUSA

ISBN-13:
978-1720788058

ISBN-10:
1720788057

Printed in the United States of America.

Preface

THE NURSERY RHYME: "Pease porridge hot, Pease porridge cold, Pease porridge in the pot Nine days old." - In those old days, they cooked in the kitchen with a big kettle that always hung on a long iron arm over the fire. Every day they lit the fire and added things to the pot. They ate mostly vegetables and did not have much meat. They would eat the stew for dinner, leaving the leftovers in the pot to get cold overnight and then start over the next day. Sometimes stew had food in it that had been there for quite a while. Hence the rhyme.

Acknowledgements

Umarex U.S.A. Air Guns
https://www.umarexusa.com

Iver Johnson Arms
https://iverjohnsonarms.com/index.html
/
Bridgford Foods Corporation
http://www.bridgford.com/

Henry Repeating Arms
https://www.henryusa.com/

Predator International Pellets
http://predatorpellets.com/

Outside The Box Outdoors
http://www.survivalistgear.com/

CHAPTER TITLE

1

Focus on Options, Not "Solutions

Steve and Beth sat on the communal beach house balcony surrounded by their friends and fellow survivors talking about the last couple days that they had spent around the marina bartering and trading for their upcoming trip back to the fish camp. It had been quite an interesting trip down to the empty lagoon house Travis, Tina and Slim had found to meet all the new people and traders while finding out about all the post-apocalyptic doings and changes on the beach around here. However, it was time to go soon as the pressing business of them trying to round up some eggs and hopefully locating a live chicken or two if someone would trade them for one needed to be seen to.

Tomorrow was Thursday and it was also the much highly anticipated day to find out if all those hand written introductory notes and sample rolls of barter toilet paper they had dropped off in all those rural mail boxes lining the road from the fish camp to here were going to pay off in trade. The barter scheme that they were depending on and had a lot of hope for was rather a simple exchange of needs affair on the surface. They had on hand an enormous available surplus of all kinds of paper goods that included toilet paper that they had scavenged from a restaurant supply truck trailer previously days before and they wanted to barter some of it for better food. This big tractor trailer sized foraging find had allowed them to have on hand a pretty good surplus of the commodity to giveaway as a promotional sales hook you might say in order to attract would be customers and hopefully have them gladly fulfill their barter request for some chicken eggs.

Tomorrow they would hopefully see if they had any willing potential takers to their proposed deal and hopefully leave them a return note to indicate if any of those country folks who were living inland had any poultry still living on their little farms. It was an iffy prospect at best, almost everyone realized that. Not too many people in these modern times still raised chickens anymore on the little land holder acreages which dotted the two-lane rural wooded highway before the collapse, chances were they wouldn't get any responses at all from their unique inquires, but they were giving it a try. The big question was if some folks still were raising yard birds at all after all this time and whether or not anyone would have any kind of a surplus that they would be willing to sell of such a rare commodity as a chicken or an egg these days. A bigger question still was would they willing to trade for such an odd mundane item like toilet paper of all things in exchange for food. This was hotly disputed topic and a gnarly bit of conjecture but it was decided unanimously by all that it was definitely worth a shot by this group of assembled survivors and those remaining live aboard boat residents of the marina that had invested in their new project.

There had been quite a share the misery party, a charitable fund raiser of sorts for the community you might say, a couple days ago that coincided with a good catch of shrimp being shared which had been brought in with the cooperation of a big passing sailing sloop. It was at this particular gathering that the matter of the boat owners sharing gas as an investment with Tavis's group and their business of undertaking this chicken eggs for a roll of toilet paper scheme had come up. The so called" Burnt Skillet" party they had conceived of to raise funds and gas with for the adventure had been fueled pretty well with the addition of some Jamaican rum donated by them but it was the Key West style beach music of a local musician named jerry Bockmuller that had been the icing on the cake if you could call it that, to get everyone's purse strings and gas can caps loosened up in the tight knit marina community. He had played one of his hit songs called "What If I Never Went Home Again" and everyone reflected on how this little piece of Florida and its community were indeed for whatever reason now, totally committed to this new Florida lifestyle of surviving and helping one another out as a group.

Focus on Options, Not "Solutions

The cakes which were served to the party goers at this little luau, that is if you want to call them lumps of dough cake, were created by Bo and Molly, the only concierge caters and cooks of the apocalypse around out of the hushpuppy mix and nacho cheese sauce that had been donated from a food scavenging trip by Travis's band of fish camp followers for the occasion. Evidently Molly had figured out how to bake a bunch of pie tins of it into the facsimile of several sizes of cake and topped them off with yummy melted cheese sauce for a highly unusual but quite inspired treat for the famished charitable party goers Travis's group was seeking donations from. For a bunch of starving folks this was ambrosia and the perfect accompaniment to a bunch of boiled fresh caught gulf shrimp.

The easy listening laid back beach music songs that Jerry was singing as the sun was going down on the Gulf of Mexico made everyone forget about their apocalyptic plights for a while as dreamy thoughts of possibly having fried chicken again someday seemed like it might materialize. This was of course totally dependent on if all of Tina and Travis's plotting and scheming paid off. The boat owners and party goers had done their share by making the old burnt up charity pot fill up with dollars for the expedition as well as donating several cans of gas to the cause in hopes of finding some hen fruit for an occasional breakfast and renew their hopes of mythical future Sunday chicken dinners.

Focus on Options, Not "Solutions

"Oh shit Molly! Here comes Frazier and Martha over there!" Bo said looking at a sixtyish couple slowly heading in their direction at the marina and it was evident that they didn't particularly care to see them today.

"What's up with them?" Tina said regarding the innocuous couple heading towards them that had their own slightly frowning looks on their faces after recognizing Bo and Molly siting nearby.

"Well, that's a kind of it couldn't be helped story if you know what I mean I need to tell you later. I guess will have to say for you to understand that they used to be former guests of our bed and breakfast that we now regret running off when the grid first went down." Molly said changing her demeanor to more of a friendly front with a strained smile and a 'Hey how are you doing' look before weakly waving in their direction.

Later on today, the survivors of the fish camp who were transplanting themselves to this area would be treated to a pretty amazing story about survival, hard feelings and ill wishes coming about from several bad decisions made by all in that bed and breakfast at the beginning of this apocalypse. It seems that elderly couple Martha and Frazier that were approaching them at a snail's pace had come down to Florida on vacation from Tennessee to spend four days at Molly's cut rate priced B&B before the poo had hit the fan and had ended up waking to some hellacious problems and very hard realities that nobody was prepared to discuss civilly it

5

seemed when the grid went down and their circumstances drastically changed. Molly had worked at home for Apple and she made extra money in the same space by renting an extra bedroom in her home for vacationing summer beach going guests when the grid was up. Quite resourceful and quite entrepreneurial.

It seems that she had known at two in the morning the very day the great disaster started that something serious was amiss. She had turned on the radio after the power in the house had went out and was shocked to hear that the nation had just experienced what was being called both a terrorist and cyber-attack on its infrastructure. These attacks had caused a major national power outage and she had gone to wake up her brother after some consideration and deliberation to explain to him that they were now in one hell of a position with these stranded guests living with them that were supposed to be checking out today. She had stayed up pondering about them until about three twenty AM that morning thinking it over and listening to an ever increasingly panicking news spokesperson talking about traffic signals being out and wrecks snarling up traffic in all the major cities before rousting her brother. Bo had said at first not to worry, that in his opinion the guests would probably just get in their car and head home as quick as they could after hearing the news themselves when they woke up. He had been kind of amazed that Frazier had advised him a couple days ago he wrote apocalyptic stories about surviving all kind of calamities for the prepper community as his science fiction niche.

Most of the time when Molly and Bo got guests to stay with them at their B&B the guests trade or occupation was pretty much unknown until the guests sometimes advised them in conversation what it was they did for a living. People stayed with them usually because of shortage of funds to stay in one of the resorts or the multi-level star and dollar accommodations at the hotels that seemed to be ever increasing in rates in these days and times. A lot of folks that could afford different just liked the experience also of sharing vacation memories at cheap abodes that they just needed to put their heads down at while the majority here lately just seemed to be former 401K retirement account zapped retirees just trying to afford a little respite from day to day hard living and have themselves a vacation of sorts.

Frazier and Martha, you might say, were all of the above but he as a prepper fiction author wanted to meet new people to study and include in his weird way as new characters in his storylines. Molly and Bo thought it was very cool to be considered to be put down as characters on the pages of some new book that would be out there forever but that didn't pay the bills and they weren't giving any kind of discount they had joked when he mentioned what he did for a living

When she had heard the world-wide power outage news She had prayed that her truck driving boyfriend might be able to make his way back to her and her brother eventually and kind of guide them in what they should do in this grid down situation and thinking like him, in Molly's opinion, this meant saving food and being in a hurry to saying goodbye and good riddance to the now nonpaying guests.

Bo at first objected to putting them out so quickly saying that old prepper dude and his wife who were staying with them had been telling him all kinds of neat stories about how o purify water and how to catch critters around here and he thought the pair might be useful to keep around awhile. However, Molly reminded him that meant sharing their food which they didn't have nearly enough of she already knew and besides they were on the coast and whatever prepper lore that old Alabama backwoodsman knew about surviving inland probably wouldn't work around here anyway.

"How so? Isn't surviving one condition pretty much just the same as surviving another? I'm sure that old guy probably knows some saltwater survival skills also! He was a soldier wasn't he and as an author writing about all kinds of survival scenarios is his gig, right?" Bo said rubbing one sleepy eye and trying to take all this in about what exactly was his position in this new state of world affairs that evidently Molly was quite righteously concerned with.

Bo was starting to snap to as he woke up this morning to hear the shocking news that the electrical grid was down, and he became even more mentally awake

8

after hearing Molly wanted him to be the one to put out the very same folks that had told him several amusing prepper stories the last few nights. He couldn't figure out why it was that Molly seemed so upset and wanted the guests out of the house right now this minute the way she was talking. He didn't understand that, she had been getting along with them fine this whole time and she had even gone ahead and showed this prepper fiction author and his wife (once she got to know them better) the AR rifle which her so-called prepper minded survivalist boyfriend had been sending packages after package to her almost daily so she could build her own rifle from scratch for some obscure reason. Frazier thought it had something to do with their fear of government gun confiscation conspiracy theories, to which Bo had just nervously laughed. He wasn't a gun guy and knew little of such survivalist fears. Molly on the other hand had just laughed at Frazier's snide observation and said it was an enjoyable experience constructing it and she just wanted to hurry up and get it done so she could shoot it. She was also being introduced to reloading and showed them a bunch of empty brass cartridges and joked about more packages coming.

Frazier had explained that from his experience with the friends he had known to take on such a project to build their own that there must be some kind of ever evolving financial trap set when it comes to folks spending all their time and money on that kind of hobby instead of just buying a stock one off the shelf and getting good with it shooting targets at the range right off the bat. He had kind of hesitated when his words were seemly falling on deaf ears and him not getting excited about looking at pretty packages and boxes of polished gun parts that did not formulate a complete working AR style rifle until sometime in the distant future.

He, got a wicked smirk that was noticed by all he disapproved of having so much expensive reloading equipment instead of active shells if you are of that mindset. Molly had argued that might be important as well as interested to reload your ammo because you could get wheel weights off of car tires to which Travis guffawed and said let's get back to this fictional story I wanted to write you into.

The next day was different however, all the fun talk about gun prepping, non-prepping the night before and how the sheeple were going to get by when all the chips were down went out the window as the true nature of this very real apocalypse became known. It seems that Molly and Bo had spent a good part of the early morning hours talking up until dawn while listening to the incoming Emergency Management reports about the grid going down and most likely staying down for an indeterminate length of time due to a supposed Korean infrastructure attack. Talking about what exactly that all meant to them personally interrupted their debating a little on exactly when they thought their house guests should leave and go home. It wasn't until it was announced that the President would address the Nation that a state of martial law was being declared by him and the Department of Homeland Security in the next hour that they went ahead and decided to go wake up the vacationing couple so that they could listen to the broadcast also.

Knock! Knock! "Yeah, what do you want?" Travis mumbled to the sound of the surprise beating on their bedroom door as Tina woke up and looked confusedly in that direction wondering what was going on.

"If you don't mind we need you both to wake up and come out here with us to listen to the news on the radio. Me and Bo want to talk to you about something important for a minute that's developing on the national front. I will wait until you wake up a bit more to tell you the rest but we got word about some really bad weather last night that is going to affect your trip home this morning." Molly said after apologizing to them profusely for having to be waking them up this early after their festivities of last night.

"We will be out there in a minute and meet you in the living room." Frazier called out as Martha got an "Oh hell!" look on her face and reluctantly started to get out of the bed to get dressed shakily.

"I thought it was supposed to be a pretty day weather-wise today!" Frazer said wondering why they had gotten this unexpected emergency wakeup call. He questioned Martha of course about this subject and she said she didn't know either, as far as she knew it was sunshine all day but Molly sure sounded serious about them getting up and getting a move on to tell them something.

"Could be that the railroad line had a hazardous spill from a wreck or something or Lord forbid, it could be that nuclear reactor over there by Dothan has got some kind of shut down or melt down problem like Fukushima had they haven't told us about yet. Whatever it is, it was important enough to them to wake us up at five friggin AM this morning so we'll know in a minute." Frazier said speculating while putting his boots on.

Frazer stared at Martha as she arched one eyebrow that basically meant "What the hell" and proceeded to put on her shoes and groggily followed Travis out to the living room to talk to Bo and Molly who were sitting in recliners waiting for them to sit on the couch.

"Morning! What's up guys?" Martha said looking at them speculatively and more than a bit worriedly before they got to the couch.

"Grid's down! Evidently, all that crap you were scaring us with in them stories last night about a solar storm or a nuke taking out the grid has in some way come true by a North Korean terrorist attack! They didn't nuke us but they blew up some key components and the radio says there is ongoing hacking or cyberwar on our infrastructure" Molly said

Focus on Options, Not "Solutions

"Oh shit! When the hell did all this happen? Sakes alive we are in for it now!" Frazier blurted out just now noticing that the AC was off and all the lights were out.

"Where all did this happen at? I mean the attacks." Martha said trying to decide to go and hug Molly on her way to look out the window at the morning dawn.

"She woke me up out of bed around 3.30 a.m. I forgot to ask you Molly what time it was when you first heard about it." Bo said looking up.

"Somewhere just after midnight is when the grid went down as near as I can tell you. That was when our power went out. Thing is it's not just our grid that's down, it appears now that most of the world's grid is down also!" Molly said meaningfully.

"Oh Crap!... Hey, this isn't a candid camera or a new Natgeo Doomsday Prepper freak the survivalist out comedy show thing that you are trying to do to me is it? Tell me you all are not trying to get even with me some kind of way for telling so many fictional apocalyptic disaster stories or referring to my SHTF books all night, are you?" Frazier asked with a halfhearted smile towards her bug eyed" Oh hell" look that told him his thoughts were no way true.

"No, boy what Molly is telling you is all true I am sorry to say. I really wish that I could say that we were messing with you and it was all a joke, but I assure you that we aren't kidding you in any way!" Bo said letting that bit of news sink in as Molly and Martha exchanged knowing glances of expected impending doom.

Martha turned towards Frazier with a shocked look on her sleepy-eyed face and said after a long heartfelt mutually confused stare, "What do we do now?"

"I don't know darling, sounds like we are in deep do do. Are ya'll sure this ain't a bunch of crap, it ain't just some hacker playing games with the media? No Orson Wells War of The Worlds radio prank going on or something? if it is I'm going to get real sore!" Frazier said looking up, knowing it wasn't any kind of prank but still hoping it was.

"No, your worst nightmare is happening for real and now it appears that we have ourselves a pressing mutual problem" Molly said.

"Sounds to me like the whole world has got a doozy of a problem!" Martha said.

"That and more!" Frazier related while struggling trying to grasp the situation.

"Uh Frazier...We have a sensitive matter we need to discuss with you and Martha. You all were supposed to be checking out of here this afternoon you remember?" Molly said leaving that last statement hanging in the air.

"I had that in the back of my mind but I need to wake up some first before thinking on it more. What are you getting at?" Frazier asked ominously thinking that her tone had changed to something that didn't sound like it was going to bode well for them in some way.

"What I am saying is that we need to discuss your departure. We need have us a conversation right now if you don't mind on what time that might be you two are leaving. What are your plans, what are you going to do now? Ok I will give you a bit longer to wake up some more before talking and choosing a time" Molly said looking like she had braced herself to be extra firm about check out time or something as she looked back at him before Bo interjected.

"What she's saying is Frazier is what are your travel plans now that you have heard the bad news about the grid going down? We kind of figured that you might want to take advantage of being up already and get an early start for home ahead of the traffic. Me and Molly have kind of been up for a little ourselves already and we have been discussing your possible plans and didn't know if you would be wanting to head back home today or not. We wanted to tell you all first that it would be o.k. for you to stay around another day or two with no charge if you thought that best. We sort of thought from what you were saying from that fictional story you were telling us last night that you might want to wait the traffic out for a day or two. I told Molly didn't think you wouldn't want to be out on the road immediately after a disaster when everyone vacationing here was leaving out all at once for safety sake maybe. I know this is a big load of bad news to drop on you all at once, but I guess what it is we are getting at is just exactly when is it that you are planning on going home?" Bo said sheepishly and looked back towards Molly for affirmation.

"Well, I just don't know how to answer that question just yet. Gives us a bit to get our wits about us and make some decisions. Molly did they say on the radio how bad things were on the highways for travel advisories?" Martha asked as she tried to consider their plight.

"Whoa now, hang on a minute we are moving too fast here! I will get around to telling everyone when it is we are leaving shortly. Tell me first though about how the radio is saying that the grid was disabled and by who. I also want to know more about what the government is saying they are doing about it and after digesting that I might be able to tell you something we all can use to get through this." Frazier said gruffly not liking to be hurried this way after just waking up and wondering what the rush was about them leaving here other than what he had heard so far.

"The president is declaring Martial Law and he will address the Nation in a half hour or so from now." Bo said looking at his watch.

"We definitely want to listen to that! I can't see them imposing any travel bans yet but I can see all kinds of folks in all kinds of government positions going crazy. Shit, I hate to be the bearer of further bad news and lay another problem on you but we are light on gas Molly. We were going to fuel up on our way out this morning but that ain't going to happen with no electricity for the pumps. You got any gas in your car that you might be willing to sell for a good cash premium? That is if you all are not bugging out of here somewhere yourselves." Frazier said pleadingly.

"Sorry Frazier, we ain't got it to spare. I am sitting on half of a tank and none of its for sale I can tell you that right now! Bo you know anyone around here that might be willing to sell them some gas? We have seen folks in situations like this before lacking fuel for a hurricane evacuation but this is a lot different." Molly said worriedly and visibly upset that they had foolishly allowed their gas tank to get so low and now it appeared leaving them stuck on her doorstep.

"I ain't got a clue who might sell them gas! Molly you know folks around here are not going to care much about helping somebody they don't know and they will be thinking about looking out for number one and their own cars. Tell you what Frazier, you and I can go door to door asking the neighbors anyway if they got any to spare but I doubt that they will sell you some at any price knowing the pumps aren't going to be coming back on line anytime soon. For that matter, I sort of doubt that any of them people are even up or out of their beds yet. I doubt most have even heard yet what's going on in the world this morning." Bo said speculating and coming up dry in regards to possibilities to get some fuel.

"That's the first priority we need to take care of. We don't even have a gas can to siphon into. Do you all have one we can borrow if we do manage find some gas? We have one of those shake siphon thingys but nothing to put fuel in." Martha said dejectedly.

"No, we don't have a gas can. Peoples yards around here are so small that folks usually pay a lawn service or use electric mowers." Molly stated.

"Bo can you get a can at work?" Molly asked.

"No, they got them all locked up, I wash the boats I don't work on them but we can go see if one of the mechanics shows up for work and maybe get one. Maybe we will be able get some gas somewhere down that way if the price is right." Bo said considering their plight.

"How much gas do you all got in your van anyway?" Molly asked pointedly.

"Only about a quarter of a tank is all. We will need to find us at least 10 gallons I am guessing, maybe more to get to a friend's house in Alabama we can stay at until we figure out if we can make it to Tennessee. But that estimate doesn't take into account how much we might need because of slow moving traffic clogging the highways or any possible detours for wrecks sucking the life out of any kind of mileage that engine can get on the highway. I would give somebody a hundred bucks in a heartbeat for ten gallons of gas if you have any ideas." Frazier said doing some mental calculations.

"You have some yourself some huge problems to solve Frazier. I suggest we give it a couple hours and then we will try the neighbors and Bo can walk up to work and see if anyone shows today. Meantime its almost time for the President's address.

My Fellow Americans it is with deep despair and a saddened heart that calls for me to speak to you today. Never before has an enemy dared launch an attack on the heartland of our great nation but at One Am Eastern standard time a deliberate unprovoked and undeclared concerted attack on our power grids and oil pipelines in the Midwest caused a cascading effect that took the power offline from the east to west coast. Our engineers and electronic technicians are working on a solution but current estimates say it will be 6 months to a year before we can restore power to most of the nation....

Focus on Options, Not "Solutions

"Well he said a mouthful but other than evoking emergency powers acts the president actually said not much of nothing." Frazier declared standing up and he and Bo went to try to buy some gas off the neighbors but returned about an hour later with no luck.

"All I can come up with is asking more random strangers to sell us some or parking next to the road with a big sign saying we need gas." Martha said.

"You want to tell him, or should I?" Molly said looking like she was bracing for a fight.

"You could have been more diplomatic and waited a few minutes!" Martha said scolding her and looking angry.

"Nothing personal, this is just as hard for me to get out in the open as it is for you all to listen to and I don't see the point in waiting any longer. Frazier I been talking to Martha and unfortunately, gas or no gas you all need to get going somewhere day after tomorrow. Maybe that will give you some time to find some fuel I hope it does but after that I can't feed or house you any longer. There I said it." Molly said hands on hips looking over at Bo for support but he was looking like he wanted to climb under a rock just about now.

Frazier looked at her shocked for a moment and fought down a bit of anger when he saw that Martha had been crying before responding.

"This is a bit sudden and I know you have your reasons that are all probably good ones but can we talk about this? Don't get me wrong we will get out of your hair as quick as we can but it might take a little longer..." Frazier began before Molly cut him off.

"Please don't make it any harder than it is asking for more time, my minds made up. It has to be this way, you of all people should understand that we need all the resources we have for ourselves and we don't want you coming back later." Molly said with a hint of warning in her voice.

"Got It! We won't be back after we leave, thanks for giving us the extra day. If you don't mind Martha and I got a lot to talk over before we go looking out looking for more gas. You are not going to change your mind and lock us out of the house, are you?" Frazier said thinking that wasn't out of the realm of possibility with this sudden change in her attitude.

"Oh, come on now! I am being as nice as I can, no I won't lock you out." Molly said in a huff and then went back to her bedroom and slammed the door.

"She won't lock you out. I am going to go talk to her, take your key with you if you want. I am real sorry

Frazier." Bo said extending his hand for a shake which Frazier returned and said "Me Too!"

"She asked for the key so she can keep it. We will be back before dark unless we find some gas" Martha said venomously and went to finish packing her suitcase.

"Well I don't know what happened while we were gone but keep that door open for me buddy." Frazier said in a whisper.

"You got it! Be careful out there" Bo responded.

"So, you all have a fight or something?" Frazier asked Martha who was busily gathering up everything in their room and wanting to load everything in the van case they did find some gas.

"No, well a little bit. She sort of hinted that you might be desperate enough to try to steal some and didn't want any trouble around her house and I said a few things but mostly we got along." Martha said giving him a quick hug and then going back to securing their luggage.

"Well she might have been just talking, she is a bit brusque about this whole business to say the least." Frazier said wondering if Molly was in her bedroom busy scrambling to get that AR rifle put together to enforce her eviction notice before dismissing it as a silly thought. The woman had been indeed had been kind enough to offer them an extra day or two too get their act together and he guessed that in her mind she was making the only decision possible and not waiting on the inevitable possible outcomes.

"So old Prepper man? What do we do now?" Martha said looking brave and fearless before melting a bit and giving him a long tearful hug.

"We go up the road by the bar and try to get some gas. The bar won't be open but somebody will be by eventually to keep it from getting looted or move stock and we try to buy booze and gas. While we are over there we talk about where we going to live around here until we can find a way out." Frazier said giving her a pat.

"Sounds like a plan to me. Let's go rule the world!" Martha said with a smile and picked up her suitcase as Frazier grabbed his and they headed out.

2

A Fine Kettle of Fish

Frazier and Martha left Molly's house the next day. Good byes were said but very little eye contact and no smiles by the departing travelers were exhibited. It just wasn't fair and not right in their opinion to be put out of the house so soon and you could cut the tension in the air with a knife. No sense staying around another day or listening to any more comments about them having to leave let alone what time that was supposed to be the couple decided. Frazier And Martha did understand Molly and Bo's reasoning and although it vexed them they begrudgingly admitted to themselves they couldn't be to mad at them for making the move to evict them so early in this disaster, but in their opinion, they certainly could have done it with less drama.

On the flip side, having two strangers living in your house at the start of the apocalypse was just too troublesome for the bed and breakfast proprietors to wrap their heads around it seemed. They were right about their decision in many respects, whatever food they had stored was going to be needed by them personally from now on and they didn't seem to see any strategic or moral reasons to team up with their elderly guests to try to survive this mess together and wanted to lone wolf it without them around in any form or fashion.

Bo and Molly had listened somewhat patiently to Frazier and Martha's objections about them not being able to remain on premises until they found the tiny bit of gas they needed to make a stab at getting home and considered vaguely the possible usefulness of having a survival expert on hand guardedly but were firm in their decision. Frazier and Martha had to go. All though they were attempting to be nice about the big mess it was evident that they had already made their minds up about them leaving post haste and nothing anyone said would change that so Frazier just said they would be gone in the morning.

Martha had begun to object that it wasn't just prepping knowledge and survival skills they had to offer but a wary cautionary look from Frazier made her drop the subject. She knew the prepper OPSEC rule of not showing all their cards. Now was not the time for full disclosure of their supplies or their intended whereabouts that they were thinking about living at.

Operations security (OPSEC) is a process that identifies critical information to determine if friendly actions can be observed by enemy intelligence, determines if information obtained by adversaries could be interpreted to be useful to them, and then executes selected measures that eliminate or reduce adversary exploitation of friendly critical information.)

In a more general sense, OPSEC is the process of protecting individual pieces of data that could be grouped together to give the bigger picture (called aggregation).

Beyond Mollie and Bo possibly knowing as preppers they had at least 72 hours' worth of food in their bug out bags and were armed with conceal carry permits the pair of innkeepers didn't have a clue what else was still stored in that van and Martha and Frazier were going to keep it that way. They talked a bit further about trading them out of gas but that conversation didn't get any further than Frazier hopefully saying "We have a little bit of silver bullion that I would like to offer if you don't want to take green cash ...." he began before Molly shut down the conversation immediately with her hand raised and clenched, saying for him not to offer her anything for what she was adamant about that she wasn't selling anything to anybody. She then began to reiterate that there was no way, no how, wasn't going to happen she would consider selling any part of what little bit she had left in precious commodities like gas or food that were soon to be slipping through her fingers so he better quit! And on that note, she fiercely voiced a reminder for them not to come back around in the coming weeks when she knew the food was going to run out her answer would be the same.

A Fine Kettle of fish

"I told you already we ain't going to be ever coming back here once we leave damn it!" Frazier snarled and both sides looked abashed and apologetic shortly their after. There was no sense in leaving permanently like this over harsh unmeant word that neither of them should have considered using. The extra unwarranted threats Frazier knew he didn't need, nor did he think it needed to be said so many times and him having to growl back but it was he guessed officially out to the jungle now and he knew its laws from years of street living. He had already considered that if they all weren't all good people things could of already went bad. Frazier could have pulled out his pistol and took what they wanted from their hosts if he was as coldblooded as he was being accused of regarding his need for gas. Hell, for that matter he should have said Bo could have murdered them in their sleep for their survival gear if abject unreasonable paranoia had taken over what were normally sane and righteous people. Sort of like it sometimes did with gold fever in prospectors No they were all normal people stuck in bad positions and everyone just soon be left alone rather than take on new challenges and hardships.

What neither Molly or Bo knew about the two now evicted refugees was just how prepped they actually were to be able to take care of themselves and maybe some other survivors come what may. The former innkeepers didn't have a clue how much survival wisdom and capabilities were now walking out their front door and they didn't seem to care, they could take care of themselves better than having two old people underfoot they figured.

A Fine Kettle of fish

This was because communications had broken down before Martha or Frazier had gotten around to revealing to Molly and Bo a few aces they had up their sleeves. The Bed and Breakfast keepers had no way of knowing that in addition to Frazier and Martha's known camping gear and bug out bags the pair of preppers had them something stored in the van something they called a "Chill Bag." This was a designed by Frazier as a special purpose built "Bug In and be safe "duffel bag which Martha jokingly called her portable pantry stuffed with MRE sandwiches and other goodies built for normally feeding four folks for 72 hours which Martha and Frazier could easily conserve and stretch into over a week of food for the themselves in addition to the other food stuffs they had on hand that they needed to take stock of. They had brought lots of snacks they hadn't gotten into for their vacation along with more of those cool Bridgford Ready to Eat Sandwiches they had purchased for the trip and hadn't gotten into because of eating out etc. Frazier and Martha liked carry them in their cargo pockets when they went on outdoor adventures because they provided an inexpensive meal solution for backpacking, camping, hunting, hiking, fishing, and boating as well as for Home Emergency Preparedness.

14 Great Tasting
Ready to Eat
Flavors
GREAT FOR LONG TERM FOOD STORAGE
NEEDS IN THE EVENT OF AN EMERGENCY

A Fine Kettle of fish

The sandwiches were a good choice as a basic staple because they typically have a lot more calories than just an MRE entrée. For example, chicken chunks only have 180 calories.

For the sake of math here we are going to round off low and call a MRE sandwich pouch 300 calories, each meal is different, for example the Pork with BBQ Sauce is 360 calories where as an Apple Turnover is 330 calories.

Now I can hear all the preppers that are going to be fussing my suggested calorie count per day is too low to be depending. No, it's not, this is called a "Chill Bag", you are supposed to be sitting around bugging in and not doing anything strenuous. Kind of like sitting in one of those now defunct Civil Defense shelters we had back in the day. The daily allowance for calories Frazier had in his bag exceeded what the so-called experts back then calculated and it was dang sure a lot tastier!

After millions of dollars and years of research, it turned out that after a nuclear apocalypse, the remnants of the American civilization would survive during the Cold War Civil Defense ERA by chowing down on whole-wheat crackers. The government dubbed its creation the "All-Purpose Survival Cracker. Plans called for shelters to stock

10,000 calories of food per person, which would have worked out to a little over 700 calories per person, per day over the expected two-week stay underground. Each government-run shelter was also to be stocked with 21-inch-tall fiberboard drums, lined with plastic, that would start out as water storage — containing just 3.5 gallons of drinking water per person for the entire duration of the internment — and then, once empty, be converted into toilets. Since there was little else to do in a shelter, the government literature encouraged serving six small single-cracker "meals" each day of precisely 125 calories. The cracker diet would also include stockpiled tins of mouth-soluble "carbohydrate supplements," i.e., suckable yellow and red hard candy. As one official explained, "Although this may seem somewhat austere, nutrition experts consider it adequate and in accord with minimal survival concept." That's a bureaucratic way of saying that the crackers would provide the equivalent of a Doomsday starvation ration — you'd still be hungry, you'd still lose weight, but you wouldn't starve to death.

Whereas I am not even counting all the extra 200 calories in the two pack tortillas that Frazier had distributed without count and stuck in every nook and cranny of his and Martha's gear. This MRE (Meal Ready to Eat) side dish contains 2 wheat flour tortillas.

A Fine Kettle of fish

Frazier was fascinated with this portable food item; the serving was rated at 220 calories and to him they were just as good as pilot crackers in nutrition almost and even better because you can put anything on a tortilla! Can of tuna, fish taco, get the pellet gun out, squirrel enchilada, use whatever you got to make you a portable meal that didn't need a plate. Martha liked them with canned deviled ham and although those little tins can add up in price as well as weight Frazier seemed to like buying a few here and there and forgetting about them in the preps. Martha on more than one occasion found her bug out gear getting pregnant with them as Frazier secretly slipped in a small tin here and there. The same with the tortillas, she had packs of them slipped into her canteen cover, tackle box you name it! Frazier mumbled something about them not weighing much but he had carried them big cans of C rations around in the army in his rucksack and when she went to the grocery store to buy them chips, candy etc. for the trip she knew she could find him on the canned meat isle buying a can or two of Spam etc. to throw in their food bag "just in case" as he was wont to do.

A Fine Kettle of fish

."

Help a fellow prepper out and buy MRE pizza and get other useful survival supplies from my buddy at http://www.survivalistgear.com/

Back to the Chill bag and calculating how much food and how manty pouches they had stuffed in that duffel at 300 calories per pouch or double that for the special civilian camping versions and we get.

Eating light for 72 hours

900 calories equal 3 pouches a day per person = one meal consisting of two pouches and a snack for later or you can have a breakfast sandwich like the Filled French Toast for breakfast and a meat sandwich like Barbecue for lunch which is a great way to start a day and then maybe eat a cinnamon roll with your coffee for dinner when you settle in for the night. Four people eating 3 pouches each a day = 12 x three days (72 hours_) 36 pouches total but the duffel contained more than that. Actually, it was a 144 hour or a 6-day bag for four the way

it was set up if that is all you ate, because it contained 72 pouches quite often if they didn't get in it on a camping trip or give samples away etc.

Eating heavy (more activity) requires 64 pouches

1800 calories equal 6 pouches a day = two full meals

Four people eating 6 pouches a day =18 x three days (72 hours_) 64 pouches

2 folks eating 900 plus calories a day or 6 pouches divided into 64 equals 10.6 days of eating for Mollie and Frazier to hold up and "Chill" for a bit away from danger.

What they had on hand personally gear wise in this come as you are standalone disaster bag besides all that chow was very enviable food foraging capabilities, particularly after the rations ran out. Molly and Bo would be missing out on every aspect of that survival wisdom and gear and if they had been more amenable probably the biggest reason they needed to keep the two old birds around. That little bit of extra gear gave Frazier and Martha survival and food gathering capabilities that were far beyond any stretch of survival imagination or fantasies Molly and Bo had on surviving on their own for the next month or so. Matter of fact the four of them could of "chilled" for a month if they hadn't got run off and not even use what Molly and Bo had in their pantry by utilizing the contents of the bag as a disaster ration extender.

A Fine Kettle of fish

This well named bag reflected Frazier and Martha's many years of prepping wisdom and lore as well as hard won practical knowledge on surviving a few long-term hurricane outages and polished by advancing age along with no romantic notions what so ever of them even considering toting giant bug out bags of A-Z prepper gear very far or for that matter ever considering needing too.

Frazier had been over the years the most influential and practical minded one in the considerations for forgoing old fanciful bug out scenarios and loads and instead began concentrating on lightening their carry loads and extending their survival capabilities mainly through his observations of his beloved Martha both physically and mentally as a fictional character in one of his apocalyptic books that he could somehow enhance with his imagination preparedness wise by applying brain over brawn. He wasn't any spring chicken himself anymore and he knew the value of not wearing yourself out physically if there was any way that he could think to get around it.

He had been shaving off bits of gear and paring down or repurposing mutually shared items from both his and his sweeties basic hit the trail backpacking gear camping loads for years. As times changed so did his model for the most practical and successful way that he could come up with so that an aging 60-year-old petite woman could somehow make hiking the long distance of maybe 60 miles without a car as a get home or get to help bag of sorts, one that would actually work. A daunting task indeed some would think but take into account she would also be most likely needing the same equipment setup as an active and capable 70 year old if they learned this senior survival bug out or bug back bag thing a bit better.

This took a lot of planning and doing as well as a few hilarious arguments and comparisons of younger folk doing the same thing because she had the packrat nature of a newbie or experienced prepper along with a C 130 cargo airplane load masters penchant for storing gear and had a bag of her own that required a lot of muscle and determination to even lift it out of the van before acknowledging defeat. This was because it contained every well imagined and closely considered Knick knack that you could ever possibly want or need to survive the zombie apocalypse and then some. She eventually reconsidered the contents of her perfect bug out bag notions once the financial ramifications and time constraint considerations of raising a mule to carry all that stuff she had accumulated became impractical and then dutifully started reducing it down to smaller bags (Whoever wrote that article five bags for survival or whatever needs to be shot!) Well she ended up with several specialized this kind of bag or that kind of emergency bag and then added more gear to them to make each one complete before she or the credit card had a nervous breakdown filing them up and then soon became frustrated and disillusioned with it all while thinking about further miniaturization before Frazier had stepped in to offer his two cents on what he thought was practical and what was not.

See the two old souls or kindred spirits had met a few years back dating when Martha had really just started gearing up on her prepping and preparing for that weird feeling or worldly inkling that something is just not right or something bad is coming that all us preppers do and to Frazier this preparation was old hat but it was still very exciting to find someone who actually liked to share his prepping passion with.

He had originally started out their love affair with each other and their mutually shared hobby by giving her some of his old extra gear to top off her preps and he had a blast talking about this or that disaster scenario and an item use for this or that end of the modern world scenario, but he quickly found out that he hadn't said nearly enough about how to lighten the load and to just carry the essentials you were actually going to need by reducing weight. They had until recently different bags scattered here and there until he started consolidating everything and working on what for a better name he called his senior survival kit.

"Lord please don't call it that or you will lose all your readers young and old!" Martha had chided him saying she objected to the mental picture of an emergency management advisory for remembering your meds or a TV commercial having something to do with financial survival.

"Well I don't know what to call it, I can't think of a cool acronym for the prepper and survivalist community at the moment to refer to like an INCH Bag (I Am Never Coming Home) That was a good way to rationalize a purpose and the perfect abbreviation to get a point across about what it was for but that's not the scenario I am trying to project and teach at the moment. Not that it matters much to me about putting a cool moniker on it because it is based on what I perceive is exactly what a particular special needs group might require in the way of gear due to physical limitations that I am thinking on. See all these young buck preppers and does out here are thinking about their physical stamina or youth to be able to make it long term in the woods or something and they are not taking into account their weakened conditions from possible starvation after just a few days having ate everything in their bug out bags. Martha you remember that you were talking to me about the likely chance or possibility of you not being able to get down to prepper shack if a solar flare took the grid out and your vans computer while you were up visiting your dad in the nursing home carrying all that camping gear you got stored in your vehicle. We discussed once that not even a military aged kid in good condition carrying a light load and a couple days' worth of food and water could make that trip because they would be falling out after that first five-mile day and slowing down a bit more from then on, most likely. Twelve days of hiking like at that rate would find you in pretty dire straits even if the blisters, physical exhaustion, sleepless mosquito filled nights, lack of food, shortage water etc. didn't get you first. That was when we came up with that nifty fold up adult kick scooter that you carry in the van. That piece of lightweight easily stowable transport would double or maybe even triple the distance that you could make in a day instead of walking and also be a big help to you to carry a load. But you don't need a load of crap, you need to get back to the house as soon as possible and that means traveling as light and as fast possible." Frazier had advised and then introduced to her to what he called his Rural Ranger rig.

The concept wasn't anything more than the old H pattern LBE (Load bearing Equipment) Alice web gear that he had experience with when he was in the Army, but it seemed to serve his needs better now for light travel than most preppers bug out bags. He had developed the system for himself years ago as a drop your pack and try to survive as long as he could way of always having his basics with him.

"Building blocks are what you need." Frazier had explained and then produced a set of military surplus web gear that he had recently purchased for Martha and while he showed her how to put it all together to wear by adjusting the straps and belt said that he would show her in a minute that this would be all she needed to make it from point A-B with maybe the addition of a small backpack to contain a superlight weight compressible sleeping bag and a bit more food and clothes maybe but he would explain about what to put in that that fanny pack later on.

"The first two things we got here are canteen covers, the old-style covers you usually see for sale cheaper are ok but the new ones have advantages so I splurged a bit and got you those. The first advantage to them is that you can store more crap in them. I am sure you like that!" Frazier said with a grin and then went on to explain that secondly it helps to conceal that your carrying a canteen on your person to the civilian survivors out there.

"You got to remember that you are going to most likely be meeting other folks on the road and that carrying an obvious canteen on your hip like the old-style ones can draw unwanted attention." Frazier explained and also advised her there are plenty of unscrupulous folks that will just say "Gimme some of that water" without the nicety of asking please and will possibly try to even take it from you by force. Wearing a military rig had its disadvantages but with a light pack on it would look like it was part of it like a waist band or something from a distance. Also, if she had assembled the Henry Survival Rifle she had and was open carrying the covers would probably look like ammo pouches to the uninitiated and they would think twice about messing with her.

A Fine Kettle of fish

"So, I keep my survival rifle in my pack until I decide it is time to open carry? How do I decide when the time is to assemble it?" Martha asked.

"When your gut or conditions tells you too. We will get into that bit of threat level assessment later. Now the number one thing you need for survival as you know is water. Water is heavy and this soldier gear will help you carry it but we are going to do it with a twist. This first pouch contains a one-quart canteen, the time to fill it up is now. The pouch also contains a canteen cup that you can use to collect and boil water as well as some water purification tabs. That is a survival system, throw your Sawyer water filter in your backpack or carry it in your butt pack whichever you prefer. Now this other pouch contains a bottle of survival tabs, that's food for 2 weeks if you have to depend on it the manufacturer says. Also, they did a very cool thing, there is a plastic bag that comes with it so you can dump out all your survival tabs into it and use the container for another 1-quart canteen. Have an extra full canteen in your pack. If your able to get clean water before you leave then do the conversion thing. Ok now with just that system if you can find more water you are good to go for 2 weeks. I have a 2-quart canteen in my pack instead of the one quart but that's my preference. A quart (32 oz) of water weighs **two pounds**. I suggest you add two pounds of food in the form of nutritionally dense MRE rations instead of carrying the extra quart of water but we see what this whole setup weighs when we are done.

Ounces equal **pounds** and **pounds** equal pain "Frazier warned.

"So, what all type of survival gear do you suggest goes in that butt pack?" Martha asked getting into the game excitedly and trying to stifle all the suggestions she had coming to mind.

"You leave that thing alone and promise me that you won't be adding anymore to it ok?" Frazer said knowing she would have it packed to the gills as soon as he turned away and commented he was watching the prepping wheels turning in her mind.

"OOOOh!" Martha playfully whined while secretly thinking of all the cool prepper gear she thought she needed to stick in that fanny pack when Frazier wasn't looking.

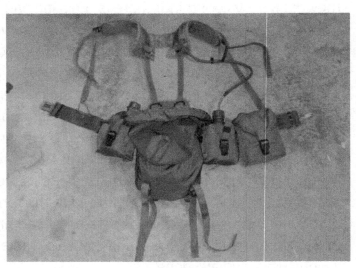

A Fine Kettle of fish

"Now there are a bazillion ways for you to rig your gear for different conditions but for now we are just talking about using it for survival and sustenance here. What do you think is next?" Frazier asked.

"PONCHO!" Martha cried with a smile, knowing Frazer thought that was the most important prep folks should have in addition to food and water.

"Exact a mundo!" Travis said with glee that all his harping on that prep had gotten through. A poncho was a prepper's best friend and he had explained overtime about a hundred uses for one other than shelter or a rain coat to her over time.

Frazier had showed her a bunch of ways for to build a shelter with one or two.

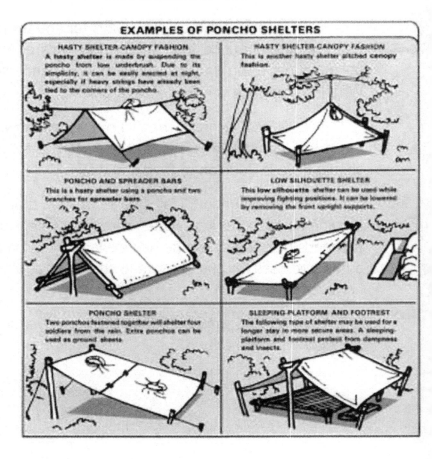

"Matter of fact when I was in the service we usually didn't have the butt packs and just folded the poncho over the belt in the back and secured it with boot blousing rubbers. You know them things that we used to keep our pants secured over the tops of our boots with in the old school Army. That way if it started raining on you while you were out in the field you could remove it from your belt easy and put your poncho on in less than a minute." Frazier explained putting the folded poncho into the butt pack.

"Ok so are you starting to see that this ain't going to be like that mobile home of a rucksack you seemed to be so determined to make a house on your back out of is it?" Frazer said joking with her.

"But there is so many needful things I might want to have along!" Martha lamented playfully but she was still thinking in the back of her mind that she could always take something out of the heavy backpack of hers if she really actually had to carry it farther than from the car to the house.

"Look I am going to make it easy on you, instead of figuring out all the crap you want to put in there you can have this instead. "Frazer said producing a Henry Survival kit.

"This has everything in it that I need in that small can?" Martha said incredulously.

"Its got a whole lot more packed in there than you think. I will go over the contents with you later." Frazier said opening it some more for a peek at the contents.

"Don't forget now you got your regular EDC (every day carry) in your pockets. Also, you can reconfigure that kit for some better items if you must but that is as big as it gets and its very complete" Frazer reminded her.

"Well I got to admit that's an awfully good survival kit but I would still like to have some other survival gear maybe stored in my back pack…" Martha began before Frazier cut her off and said light and fast was the way to go if she was to survive. He then reminded her of how folks should calculate the weight of their bug out bags.

- o A loaded backpacking pack should not weigh more than about 20 percent of your body weight. (If you weigh 150 pounds, your pack should not exceed 30 pounds for backpacking.)

- o A loaded day hiking pack should not weigh more than about 10 percent of your body weight. (If you weigh 150 pounds, your pack should not exceed 15 pounds for hiking or just a get home bag.)

"Wow I already greatly exceed that, and don't fuss at me that old bug out bag of yours I know weighs over 45lbs if you say it don't." Martha chided.

"Well in that respect I am like you and I too like to have a bunch of gear packed but I ain't planning on humping that ruck any distance I can tell you that right now. I did try to minimalize and maximize usability but even trimming extras it weighs, what it weighs and it only has 72 hours' worth of food in it. Now then back to what we were discussing, actually with this butt pack set up you are going to see that you can even get away with not having a backpack at all if conditions warranted it. Check out what my research has as an example of one of the better ways for filling up a butt pack." Frazier said showing her an excerpt.

A group called http://www.combatreform.org/ suggests the following as a **Live** Combat Light Package buttpack This is all you need to survive from the elements from freezing to 100+ degrees

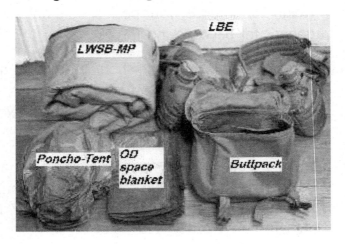

a. Army standard NSN 8405-01-416-6216 Eco-Tat Lightweight Sleeping Bag Multi-Purpose LWSB-MP (3.0 lbs.)

b. Army standard NSN 8405-00-290-0550 Poncho with 550 cords to be a poncho-tent, hood tied into a knot (1.3 lbs.)

c. Army standard NSN 7210-00-935-6665 OD Green space casualty blanket (0.6 lbs.)

d. Army standard NSN 8415-01-228-1312
ECWCS *Gore-Tex* jacket (1.5 lbs.)

6.4 pounds TOTAL

Also, in your buttpack would be a VERY SMALL HYGIENE KIT in zip-lock plastic bag:

2 pairs wool socks rolled up with small can foot powder

Moleskin for blisters

2 Pair of underwear

small travel toothbrush or one with handle cut

small bar of soap

bandanna

Toilet Paper

"Now then that web gear itself weighs something. So, does a backpack. A lot of times an empty backpack itself with a frame weighs about 4lbs so you got to figure that in before loading stuff. That leaves you very little in weight to put in that rucksack especially if you start counting your survival rifle, 380 daily carry pistol, ammo, sheath knife etc. so your pushing limits adding anything other than a change of clothes and more food. Hell, I considered, if I had any sense I could ditch 20lbs of gear out of my own personal bug out bag and be better off adding 20lbs of food. At our age I think that makes a lot more sense and I ain't bugging out to no woods anyway if we can possibly avoid it. I think that's the easy part to imagine, more food means longer and easier short-term survival while you stay indoors. It's all about reducing the need to feed and exposing yourself to danger or having to burn up calories to get calories." Frazier said before telling her how he was going to be revamping all his gear so it made more sense for the changing times and his aging body. Going Indian he suggested calling it. Getting by with less and traveling quicker and faster if need be. Instead of an Indian pony they cad their collapsible adult sized scooters to make a fast get away from a traffic jam or use to go out scouting for grub with.

The bulk of their heavy camping gear like tent, cook pots, extra food etc. he had already transferred to big duffle dry bag for use on the kayak or to carry between them by grasping a handle each. Frazier could carry it himself and his bug out bag, he just couldn't carry it very far or for very long and he was getting older by the day. He also knew what strength that he had before a disaster hit would diminish as his food intake went down and the rigors of the disaster wore him further down. This was his" we will survive no matter what or where bag." A set up that would work the same in the backyard or for that matter on the side of the road in the woods for survival. Backyard bush craft was his crafty new focus, sometimes he called it his homeless hand bag because with it in a disaster they would never be homeless or starving and they could both carry the one bag if need be when they were too wore out to carry anything else.

Guide Gear Dry Duffel Bag

A Fine Kettle of fish

French Military Surplus Tent

Poncho Liner

A Fine Kettle of fish

Clear Sheet plastic

Silky Big Boy Saw

Cold Steel Machete Bowie

Sawyer Water Filter

A Fine Kettle of fish

Ranger Squad Mess kit

Iver Johnson foldable 20-gauge

2 Quart Canteen

A Fine Kettle of fish

Crossman 1377 pistol with optional stock   Swiss
Surplus shoulder bags Yo-Yo fishing reels

A Fine Kettle of fish

Half Dozen of Each   Trap Bait
Bird Seed Blocks and Holder (Tractor Supply)

A Fine Kettle of fish

24 Gauge Brass Snare Wire   Monofilament 12lb test
Cargo cord 2000lb test (Deer Snares)

Bird Mist net   Assorted MRE
peanut butter for bait and personal use

One specialized emergency bag was purposely created by Frazier so that the two older or for that matter any two younger people could carry it between them sharing the handles and load comfortably pretty much anywhere and one that could also provide them long term survival and mobility if lord forbid they had to grab it and go. It contained around 16 lbs. of food that they knew would get lighter all too quickly as the days passed. They could make it lighter to carry even still more if necessary or if they wanted to add more food to sit in place longer by taking out the Ranger squad aluminum cooking pots. However, they had decided on this original balance of food and gear by considering when staying in place, they needed to, purify fresh water by boiling, desalinate saltwater by distillation, collect water from rain, build a solar ground still for water collection, cook a bunch of wild greens with a big rabbit and needed a large stew pot etc. They after not much deliberation settled on the notion the size of them pots were sure handy and a nice sized skillet was a dream to have along so they stayed packed in the bag. Plus, you got all that pretty much waterproof storage space in it for adding things like high energy drink mixes, spices, cocoa mix etc. Yea more weight but easily adjustable and practical. By always having this chill-out bag fully stocked with food at the ready, they could sit, eat, drink and wait comfortably on hopefully danger to pass them by for a pretty good period most anywhere. That bag clutched between them and having nothing more than a hotel room and in the worst-case scenario just the clothes on their backs allowed them to became a force to be reckoned with that didn't even have to even emerge much outside for weeks. Come knocking at the door and being a threat? That Iver Johnson 20 gauge could take down any game in North America as well as any two-legged predators that didn't want to act right. Travis could fold it up in his back pack and carry it with him hunting. That air gun of his was plenty for small game but to get a deer or protect yourself from a rabid feral dog you can't beat an Iver Johnson 700. It also diversified his hunting practices, if you were sit hunting a bunch of squirrels and a deer came along you could easily alternate between weapons.

The bag had all your basics of living in a disaster long or short term right down to an amazing little collapsible stove that only needed twigs to heat up your dinner or purify water. This was a big advantage when it came to gathering firewood or combustible biomass material like pine cones etc. in a backyard situation or some vacation spot they found themselves in.

A Fine Kettle of fish

Silver Fire Scout (Tell the owner Todd, Ron Foster recommended it to you!)

THE C>O>B> duffel also contained three solar powered inflatable LED lamps

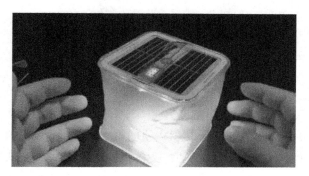

Frazier had also put a lot of thought and effort in what was needful and what was not if you had to carry it any distance in a grid down setting requiring mobility and stealth and he was a bit chagrined by the fact that the cheapest rifle in his arsenal was actually the only one he wanted or needed if he was ever reduced to sheer survival hunting when depending on one gun or one survival tool to feed him and others. 75 BBs in the reservoir, that's what I am talking about! That's what the Umarex NXG APX that was stored with in his van along with his get home bag, but it could also shoot .177 cal pellets of which he kept a ready supply of in a pocket on his hunting bag.

This wasn't anything but a swiss Military Surplus Nylon Canvas Shoulder Bag that could be used for a game bag to put squirrels and such in. It held his leather belt pouch for his pellets until he needed to attach it to his belt.

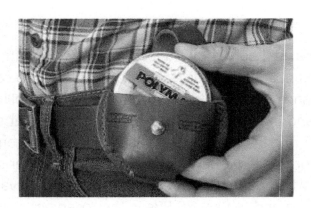

He liked the APX rifles dual ammo capability of shooting pellets or BBs and stored both to take advantage of its multi pump capability's. The Next Generation APX from Umarex USA is the genesis of modern youth air rifles.

A Fine Kettle of fish

It redefines the standard of air guns designed for younger and small-framed shooters. Even though its targeted at younger shooters it works fine for adults and is particularly use for preppers and fulfilling Frazier's needs. At 800 FPS it matched the old Daisy 880 he grew up with and that was plenty powerful enough for hunting small game. The APX however had all kinds of modern advancements its predecessor did not.

A Fine Kettle of fish

Cheap, light and accurate he didn't think he would have too big of a heart attack if someone stole it out of his van, that is unless it was stolen during a disaster! Then one of his biggest edges on surviving better than most folks would be sorely missed. He had no intentions of losing it then and it was to be jealously guarded during those times and most likely would be near his side somewhere at all times. Umarex has cleverly designed their NXG APX air rifle so it avoids the loading issue many other multi-pump dual-ammo guns have: Jamming when used with pellets because of the EZ-Load pellet ramp. Now, you can load the ammo of your choice and be assured of flawless loading and shooting. The EZ-Load pellet ramp is a feature also found only on Umarex pneumatic air rifles. The trouble-free design greatly reduces dropped or incorrectly loaded pellets.

He still had his modern survival snare set as well as a bunch of other snares and traps at his house of course. One neat thing about that air rifle he had found was it was plenty powerful to be used as a good dispatch gun for his trapline. A light air rifle can be used as a standoff way of taking the life of an animal humanely when caught in a snare. The Emergency snare kit he had came along with them for long trips near woodlands like the one they had now and didn't weigh much but he could do without them and just use what was in his chill out bag if need be. As a matter of fact, in some ways what was in that bag was much more dependable to get dinner than modern aircraft cable snares that can become twisted and useless after just one catch. Besides it's a lot easier to bait a bunch of rat traps with peanut butter for squirrels or mouse traps for birds than it was trying to lay sets for a possum or passing racoon he might not have the woodland to draw game from. Backyards have squirrels, sometimes rabbits and assuredly birds everywhere!

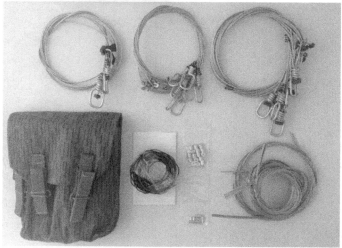

Making primitive bird traps is time consuming and their catch rate is not that high. His BB/pellet rifle could easily be deployed to feed himself with. The Umarex APX adjustable rear sight and fiber optic front sight protected by its sleek muzzle brake allows you to quickly zero in on your intended target when shooting either pellets or steel BBs. Mounting a scope to the APX is easy with its integrated tactical-style scope mounting rail system- another first in youth air rifles that provides a positive lock down to keep a scope on zero. All of these features combine to make shooting the Umarex Next Generation APX a target-busting experience for shooters of many ages.

The Predator PolyMags were is hunting ammo of choice but his " Chill Bag" held all kinds of extra ammo in cheaper more affordable flavors.

A Fine Kettle of fish

Pointed 22 Pellets

The patented Predator Polymag is a premium quality hunting pellet which combines a hollow head with a sharp polymer tip for unsurpassed performance on small game. Whether ridding your garden of unwanted pests or stalking your favorite hardwoods in search of squirrel, experience excellent accuracy and efficiency when hunting with premium Predator Polymag hunting pellets.

The Predator Polymag was designed specifically to be the most effective and efficient air gun hunting ammunition available. To accomplish this goal, the following features were incorporated into the design:

The Innovative Head Design
The hollow head with sharp polymer tip delivers maximum penetration and shock to vital organs. With instant expansion on impact, the Predator Polymag cuts and shatters bone on contact.

The Lightweight, Aerodynamic Body
Offering excellent flight characteristics, the high ballistic coefficient allows for higher retained velocity and flat trajectory. The Predator Polymag allows the hunter to take game efficiently with match grade accuracy.

The Metalmag offer the same unique hollow head design as the Polymag with a hard metal tip. This metal tip is perfect for those harder to take down crows, armadillos and larger critters. Match grade accuracy combined with the hard-hitting impact of the metal tips makes this the perfect larger critter hunting pellet.

Now for constancy and quality you can't beat Umarex steel BBs. Frazier liked the size of the container on these also. He could easily fit a small bottle in is hunting or survival vest and was secure in the knowledge he was going to be eating for a long time to come at a fraction of the weight of three bricks of 22 caliber which would require a totally different carry arrangement. Besides you ain't going to be shooting no little bitty bird in your backyard with a .22, far too loud and far too dangerous for the neighbors! That's not even considering what a bloody mess of ruined meat you might be lucky enough to end up with after performing the task successfully. With a multi pump BB gun like the UMAREX APX you can adjust the power of your shot at will and use just the right amount force while putting it accurately where you need it.

Air gun writer Tom Gaylord (The Godfather of Air guns) considers multi-pump rifles to be one of the best ways to introduce men, women and children to the shooting sports. Many air guns require more effort to cock than some shooters can exert not so the APX. With a multi-pump, the gun accommodates the shooter. It's an ideal format for a good shooting experience. It also slows things down for a new person, as a rapid-fire gun isn't a good first experience

Another thing for one to consider is that marksmanship is a skill that deteriorates over time. When the poo hits the fan is not the time to find out you have lost a lot of skills that you will have difficulty regaining especially when ammo is short and it's not advisable to target shoot because of the noise factor or otherwise for you try to get out and plink away. Cheap, accurate, durable pump air rifles like the APX can sharpen your existing skills cheaply and keep them honed while giving you hours of safe enjoyment plinking on any back lot you can find. This will give you the edge in any grid down situation to be familiar and accurate with your weapon and you and your pocket book can laugh next time we have a 22-ammo shortage. You can always find pellets and BBs anywhere! I will tell you anther secret, it's easy to break the prepper hoarding ammo habit when for 20 bucks you can get 6,000 rounds of BBs and some pellets to figure out that if you managed to shoot three birds or squirrels a day with that "not a toy" air gun that you could last for years and be eating with less room taken up than the contents of most women's purses for your ammo stockpile.

3

Razzmatazz

Frazer and Martha drove up to the corner after hurriedly leaving Molly ad Bo's house and parked in old beach bars big parking lot facing the road. Frazier turned the key off after glancing at the gas gauge one more time and sighing wistfully. He turned and looked at Martha who was deep in thought while eying the road.

"What time is it sweetie?" Frazier asked as he opened up the door to allow some fresh air in."

"Eight twenty. There is not as much traffic out here as I figured there would be." Martha said remarking on the fact they had only seen a few cars today from their short drive over here.

"Well it's still early I guess. From the traffic we saw moving around and filling up the roads yesterday I think the whole population of tourists headed out all through the night." Frazier replied.

"You sort of predicated that, are we doing the sign thing today?" Martha said referring the windshield sized cardboard "Have Money! Need Gas! "sign lying on the backseat.

"May as well but let's not drag the sign out until we figure out a few things. We are about as prepped as we could ever hope to be this far from home, we got roughly $300.00 between us and as far as I am concerned we need to try to spend it today. We ARE going to find some gas today but I have no idea what we are going to be paying. When we get our gas, we can try to head out to Marshal's house in Alabama but as you know that is a roll of the dice last ditch option. I know him a Marjorie would take us in no questions but they got a small house, small acreage and are going to be struggling hard enough themselves. I am guessing they might have 6 months' worth of food on hand and their place ain't self-sufficient at all with that tiny garden they have. I am thinking we just stay around here, that ocean can feed us and I don't think that little speck of woods they live on can." Frazier said bringing back up the subjects they discussed yesterday.

"I agree, we will probably be much better off here but the timing sucks as you already said. A lot of Folks still have plenty of food on hand and if the grocery store isn't wiped out already it will be today. I still think we should have gone to the one up the street this morning but we can work our way back as you mentioned and hit them around noon. I figured this bar might be open but I guess they sold off the majority of their liquor stock yesterday." Martha said after her and Frazier had been surprised to see the Bar/package store doing a booming business yesterday. The prices they were charging for booze had not changed from normal retail. The locals they had talked to had said the owners didn't price gouge and kind of emptied the place out like that every hurricane evacuation and normally took about three days once an emergency was declared. This time was different though, people were buying what they could and leaving. They weren't hanging around to have a few drinks and talk about the weather and such. Frazier and Martha had eyed the smaller pint bottles as barter material for later but they opted instead on two half gallons of their favorite personal use whiskey and four quarts of cheap vodka. They had two drinks in the bar each trying to hustle gas and get news or some help but no luck. Folks were worried and worried folk don't sell gas or food it seems and weren't too nice about being asked quite often.

"Shit, I sure do wish the hell Molly and Bo could have realized that four people function better than two in this early part of a disaster situation. Ass holes! That fact is particularly true if you ask me when everyone staying in one house is supposedly a prepper but that's all hindsight now. Damn! I figured this bar would be open this morning but there is no telling how long that the end of the world party lasted they had going on past sundown when we left. I hate to go all the way down to Laguna beach today and back but it can't be helped." Frazier said thinking they only had enough gas to go from one end of Panama City beach to the other maybe 3 or 4 times and there was still the matter of them locating somewhere to try to ride out the bad times ahead.

The plan was for them to try the many scooter and moped rental places dotting the beach road as well as the construction equipment rental shops in that direction for some fuel but they figured that a lot of folks had already thought of those particular targets and their chances of obtaining any gas from them would be slim. Walmart was located down that way as well as a particular small locally owned grocery store that mostly served the small community around it and they thought that they had a decent chance of being open and having something left in it. They would give Wally world a shot if it looked like they could get in and the parking lot wasn't over run. All the big chain grocery stores were on this end of the beach and they decided to just avoid the pandemonium and heavy traffic that most likely started early they suspected in that direction. The plan for this morning was to play "Rice and Bean "foraging farmers" the best they could attempting to buy said commodities from any closed restaurants that might have an owner or worker on premises that they could hopefully convince to sell them some.

"I say we go play orient express and drive around to all the Asian restaurants, I think your idea of us possibly finding some 50 lb. sacks of rice for sale might be easier for us to locate over there." Martha said wanting to move on.

"In a minute, I am watching these restaurants in front of us for signs of life. I am still wondering why all the cop cars were over at the Marina this morning. I didn't see any kind of fire or a wreck or anything. I wonder how long the police are going to stay on duty? We got to be careful not to run afoul of them no matter what and us being homeless right at the moment ain't going to help matters any." Frazier groused.

Usually during the summer months, the small seafood restaurants he had been eying had staff arriving early to prep for the lunch crowd and you would think that in a disaster like this they would have other things to do. He was surprised that he hadn't seen anybody opening up over there to empty out the non-working freezers and salvaging what they could before all that shrimp and stuff started thawing etc. Frazier wanted in on that clean out and figured it was a good place to possibly score some free perishable food that could be eaten now and if he was lucky, give him a chance to possibly buy a sack of some kind of beans or rice maybe but that plan wasn't working.

"Had the owners already completed that task yesterday?" He wondered to himself.

"Frazier, I didn't even think about us needing to campout in the van last night near likely places that would be cleaning out walk in freezers and such until you mentioned it last night. I am agreeing with you folks probably be doing the same thing tomorrow. All that frozen food stuff would probably take at least three days to defrost so there is no telling what time the owners are going to get around to doing it. I say in our case the early bird gets the worm and we need to be out on the road so we can just run up on somebody somewhere emptying out one of those defunct restaurants. We need to go to all the restaurants in this area as quick as we can and see what they will sell us in nonperishable goods and forget about hunting excess melting charitable stuff that they might give us some of. Even though your idea of the seafood places is a cool way for us to conserve on food and maybe have a free fresh meal today that limits us too much. Let's just get going exploring the neighborhood and find something to add to our preps while we can!" Martha said thinking that this peninsula was going to be smelling like the world's biggest barbecue pit soon enough as every homeowner facing the same non-powered freezer and melting food issues would soon be doing the same thing and getting the outdoor grills going.

Be the best beach bums they could be and go with the flow before the chaos hit in earnest was their new survival strategy for now. Try to run up on churches or community cook outs, wander around condo clusters in hopes of an invitation for a hand out. They weren't going to be out begging, they were just going to position themselves as best they could for taking advantage of the largesse quantity of surplus food that appears in modern society when the power goes out. Hopefully maybe even meet a new friend or two. Frazier knew from experience with disasters like hurricanes this was he time folks were most community oriented and charitable. He and Martha were in survival mode from now on and that meant them taking advantage of anything and everything that could help them save on their food stores and hold them back for another day.

They would bum around, hangout and blend into the remaining enclaves of survivors for a week or so and then figure out where they thought it was best for them to somewhat safely ride out the societal chaos they were sure at some point would commence. The would bug in and chill, stay off the streets and stay away from the looting, although Frazier was a bit contentious on that looting bit. There were times opportunity might be safe enough to approach, certainly an awareness and possible distant observation of such would be vital survival knowledge in the months to come. During the next week they should be looking for a vacant house or something they could maybe move into. They needed to think permanency as well as how long this slow starvation societal breakdown thing was going to last. Tonight, though they would probably be sleeping at the state park, Frazier had his doubts if it was still staffed and if asked they were going to say the had a payed reservation there already. It wasn't like a park ranger could check the internet anymore to confirm it. They would check out the possibility of short term campgrounds later this afternoon.

That was a mighty interesting area to check out for short term or resource for long-term living and needed further investigating.

"Ok times a wasting, let's go get out on the road and see what we can see." Frazier said cranking up the van and backing out.

"Have you thought anymore on where is it that we are going to locate to in a week or so?" Martha asked.

"I been thinking on that on and off. The golf course was the first thing that came to mind. but I don't figure that's very safe for very long even if you got off back in the woods on the fringes of it. There are a lot of high end rich folks houses close to the greens at that one closest to us to from here. I would imagine that a bunch of those folks might start thinking about hunting deer or alligators or something on the golf course quicker than waiting on their food to run out to try. That is kind of a timing thing, right now I would like to be taking advantage of all those tame squirrels and semi tame deer. I had considered hunting and camping over there for next week or so and thinning out the easy game population but that can wait a bit. We need to be near fresh water of some kind because I bet there won't even be a trickle in the pipes in a day or two." Frazier said slowing the van to eye a strip mall whole being very careful with the brakes I order not to slosh the big cooler full of water he had in the back that they had filled at Molly's house before their departure.

"There sure is not a lot of people out on the streets today! I guess most local folks are staying home and the tourists have already left mostly." Martha said eying a big closed gas station and convenience store and wondering how long it would be until people considered looting. Frazier told her that was the million-dollar question he wanted to know because they needed to try to be bunkered in somewhere when the mayhem started. He said that his best guess was 2 weeks but you can never tell what might trigger it on a large scale. Mob mentality would start in the poorer neighborhoods first he reckoned. When looting became a free for all and everyone was involved instead of random acts of thievery, that was when shit had it the fan. Anything interesting business wise that was outlying, off the beaten track or path etc. would get visited sporadically of course for burglary because the alarms were off. it was all going to depend on how much of a police presence was out physically paroling. Cops would be out for sometime he assured her but their focus couldn't last long as the shops needing guarding and opening their doors would soon be sold out of everything and they would be running low on gas.

They had both seen in their lifetimes many times the old familiar empty shelves appearance of stores within hours of a hurricane declaration. The majority of it was caused by folks waiting until the last minute preceding a hurricane to panic buy instead of building up their emergency supplies before needed. Those kinds of people were one reason that they hadn't even bothered going over by the big grocery stores not far from Molly's place. Too frantic and too crazy! Frazier said that most likely the business owners on this beach road they were on would go with what they know and be busy trying to board up their shops like a Cat 5 hurricane was predicted to make landfall there and be screwing on hurricane shutters and sheets of precut plyboard but who was to say? That a lot of the owners would be doing the customary preparedness and damage control measure they figured was a given. That was big part of why they were out and about on this side of the beach today. Frazier had brought up the question of wondering where all those carpenters were at with battery operated screw guns that appeared like army ants before a storm and could should be mobilizing around here today if he guessed correctly. He didn't think they would all remain home and he was right. Up ahead he saw five guys going to town boarding up The Wong Lee restaurant's glass windows and he pulled over quickly and got out with Martha.

"Morning! Is the restaurant's owner around?" Frazier asked a gray bearded heavy-set man marking some sheets of plyboard on the saw horses.

"He was here a minute ago, he is gone now and said that he would be back here in an hour." The man said hardly looking up from his work to acknowledge their presence.

"Mind if we wait around for him here?" Martha asked with a smile.

"Suit yourself." The man grumbled his voice barely discernable over the noise of the other workers screw guns securing wood to the window frames at a record pace.

"Hey buddy we are a little in need of some help here and want to ask you a favor. Would you mind selling us some of that gas you got for your generator?" Frazier questioned.

"You are about the third danged person that asked me that this morning." The man said looking up from his work not too pleased to be asked again evidently.

"We ain't got none to spare mister. We have several jobs we need to get done today and the business owners are paying us big money for us to get out here and do it." The man said resuming his work.

"I bet they are! I would be charging them more too considering you can't replace that gas you need for your saw anytime soon. But hey! I wouldn't myself mind paying a bit more of premium for it. We really need some bad." Frazier said hopefully.

"You can't afford it." The man said eying them shrewdly and looking over at their older vehicle.

"Well maybe we can, what are you asking for it?" Frazier said speculatively.

"I want 20 bucks a gallon for one of them 5-gallon cans and not a penny less." The man said firmly pointing towards a trailer with about 6 plastic jerry cans hanging on its sides.

"Damn you are sure proud of that stuff." Frazier said in shock.

"That's my price, take it or leave it. I hope you do leave it, that way I will probably get more for it from somebody else come tomorrow." The man said with his hands-on hips waiting to see if Frazier was going to take the deal or not.

"Does that include the can?" Martha said with a wry disarming smile and making sure it got included in that outrageous price.

"For you lady, sure, no problem, you can have the can." The man responded with a smile and put his handout to receive a $100 bill from Frazier who looked none too happy about the exchange.

"You got a spout?" Frazier asked hopefully.

"If you want to use it here I do, otherwise no." the Man said as one of the other workers walked over.

"Don't be selling no more of our gas Ralph, we are going to need it ourselves." The man said complaining.

"I am just helping some old folks out and making a few bucks in the process. That's the last can I will let go of though, tell everybody else no more gas sales today. Be nice to these folks and give them a hand with it Cletus if you would and dump it in their tank for them." The older carpenter said to the younger one and then he went over casually to crank up his generator and commenced to cutting out wood shutters for the windows.

After Cletus had got done filling their tank Frazier had to inform him that the gas can was part of the deal he had cut with the older dude to which Cletus just made a face and shoved it back at them before going back to work.

"Dang baby you took that guys deal to quick." Frazier said once they got back in the van.

"I doubt he would have taken anything less than a hundred." Martha retorted.

"No but he might have taken something else like $50 and a bottle of Vodka!" Frazier said already starting to sweat profusely on this hot Florida morning.

"I didn't think about that. You want to try waiting on this restaurant's owner or do you want to keep looking around? "Martha asked after telling Frazier she had looked at that gas deal as a bird in the hand type thing and they had paid what they had too.

"There is one of those little China express take out joints up on the next corner lets go try our luck there, no wait a minute, isn't there some kind of Louisiana or Cajun diner off this side road heading back towards back beach road? "Frazier questioned.

"Yea there is! Kind of a beat up wooden dive looking place, let's go there first!" Martha said thinking it was a likely prospect.

Frazier drove down to the seedy looking old paint peeling wooden structure and noted two pickup trucks being loaded up in the rear and pulled in.

"let me do most of the talking this time Martha!" Frazier commented.

"I will, just remember we need supplies now and there won't be none to be had for any price you would be willing to pay soon enough." Martha reminded him.

"Hey how you doing!" Frazier called out to a man exiting the back of the restaurant/bar.

"We ok! You want to buy some beer? Its $6 a six pack for domestic and $10 for import since you standing here." A heavily mustached man said with a roguish Cajun accent.

"We will drink a beer with you at those neighborly prices, I assume the bars not open." Frazier said as Martha eyed him sideways wondering what he was thinking.

"No, we had us a big blow out shindig yesterday and I guess now I am closing up for good today. I figured that was why you all stopped by was to see if I would sell any beer." The man who now introduced himself as Pierre said.

"Well sort of, Boudreaux said you might be willing to sell us some rice and beans if you had any left." Frazier said as Martha looked the other way wondering what kind of deception Frazier was going to try to pull off.

"I might have a little bag or two I could let go for a price. Which Boudreaux do you mean sent you here? "Pierre asked eying him.

"I never could pronounce his last right, the one that always goes to the Beach House Bar that is married to a nurse lady." Frazier hazarded.

"Oh! Thibodaux, he be down here last night trying to drink up all my good Barbados rum. I wish he not be so free with the selling advice for me but he friend of Pierre and that makes Pierre friend of yours. I don't have much to sell you but I make you bon champs deal on one 50lb bag of rice and one 25lb bag of red beans for $75. You see Boudreaux and that family of his done hit me up and that is all she has left to spare if you going to be a taker at my price. I make it Lagniappe and through in some rue mix and seasonings so you don't have to eat it dry Mon Ami." Pierre said with a smile.

"That's a good deal and you're a good man to help us out like that!" Frazier said getting his wallet out.

"Hold on now, wait a minute mon Grand-père (good grandfather) why do you have Tennessee plates on your van?" Pierre said eying Frazier.

"That's our sons van who is stationed over at the Navy base. We borrowed his van to come pick up the rice and beans." Martha said seeing that Frazier was having trouble and struggling coming up with a plausible excuse quick enough for not having Florida plates.

"Oh, I see, I tell Boudreaux last night I only have time for helping local people who are friends. I dunno what all them Canadians visiting down here going to do but not my business. You pull your van over here and we get you loaded up." Pierre said and Frazier was glad that most of their preps were out of sight under a movers blanket.

"You find some gas?" Pierre said raising one eyebrow at the big red gas can sitting in back of the van.

"No, that can is empty, we are looking for some though. You got any to sell" Frazier replied as he was closing the door.

"I can't help you there, I tell my kids over and over never let their cars get under half a tank and none of them listen. I bet they wish they listen to me now!" Pierre said before shaking Frazier's hand goodbye and holding Martha's hand a second before saying "Laissez les bon temps roulez! "Which is a Cajun French phrase that is literally translated from the English expression "Let the good times roll!" To which she repeated the popular phrase back to him as a farewell and began walking towards her side of the van.

"Who the hell is Boudreaux?" Martha whispered as they exited the parking lot.

"Hell, I don't know, you get around a bunch of Cajuns it seems there is always somebody named Boudreaux somewhere!" Frazier said with a laugh before admitting he had actually bumped into someone with that name awhile back at that particular bar and had just winged it.

"Well aren't you the sneaky one! I swear sometimes you are wiser than a tree full of owls! Ha I wonder if that saying a familiar name thing works at Chinese restaurants also!" Martha said with a grin as they went back to exploring.

.

Good Golly Miss Molly

It had been almost 6 hard lean months now since Frazier and Martha had wound up by themselves homeless and trying to live on these dirty streets with an apocalypse going on and although they looked pretty gaunt, dirty and tired they had fared fairly well it seemed. That was debatable of course, it all depended on who you were comparing too but to say they fared better than most was an understatement. But by the looks of them they were far from dead and somehow, they seemed to have managed this day to day root hog or die existence fairly well in spite of encountering more than their fair share of hardships. However, it got harder and harder for them every day and they were completely out of any kind of basic supplies again. The Marina was the only place they knew of to trade for flour etc. so here they were. Seeing their former hosts and rivals Molly and Bo sitting there at the table had taken them somewhat aback but they sort of expected it.

They had seen the pair before two or three times at the marina trying to trade and the strained relationship between them hadn't got any better with time or chance encounters.

"Hello Martha, Hi Frazier!" Bo said not rising from his seat to meet the couple who would probably just nod at them and walk on by them anyway.

"Hi Bo, Hi Molly." Martha acknowledged them and Frazier nodded his usual dismissive greetings back as they paused to stand before them to speak this time. Martha had her 22-survival rifle in one hand and Frazier carried his single shot gun slung over his shoulder. Travis and Tina had slowly become used to strangers coming and going from the marina open carrying guns but they had never been so close to four people all carrying guns with evident bad blood or something else between them and it made them quite nervous.

"Is Captain Vic around?" Frazier asked before introducing he and his wife to the strangers and sort of ignoring Molly and Bo.

"He was around earlier. Here comes Billie Lee and Harvey, they will know where he is at." Travis offered.

"I was sort of hoping not to see them two before I got our business done with Captain Vic. I swear that Harvey and Billy Lee are like getting gum stuck on your shoe when it comes to them trying to wheedle a commission out of someone around here." Frazier said.

"They can be a bit pesky." Tina agreed and the group waited for the pair of would be scroungers to finish walking over.

"Hello folks. Hi Martha, Frazier, you haven't been here for a visit in a long time. I am glad to see you!" Harvey said reaching out shake Frazier's hand.

"Ain't had nothing to trade so no reason to come by. Hey do you know where Captain Vic is?" Frazier asked.

"He is on his boat or visiting with a neighbor. What you need him for? Maybe I can make you a better trade." Harvey said hopefully.

"I didn't say I had anything to trade, matter of fact I want to borrow something off him." Frazier said and smiled a bit at Harvey's discomfort in finding out he couldn't profit from the visitors in some way.

"Like I said he over at the end of the dock somewhere. What do you want to borrow if you don't mind me asking?" Harvey said not willing to give up on a possible sales lead so easily.

"I want to borrow that little red wagon of his if you must know." Frazier said referring to the child's Radio flyer wagon Vic used to move stuff up and down the dock sometimes.

Martha was grinning like she was going to bust as Harvey and Billie Lee tried to find words to find out what was going in that wagon without showing too much interest.

"We can tote whatever it is you want to carry in that wagon and it will hardly cost you a cent!" Billy Lee offered.

"Nah thanks for the offer buddy but Captain Vic is going to have to tote it himself." Frazier said and Martha and he turned to walk down to the docks.

"We will go down there with you, he might want some help from us!" Harvey offered.

"He might I will ask him for you after I talk to him." Martha said advising them this was a private conversation and she and Frazier walked down the sidewalk towards the docks alone.

"What do you suppose they want to carry in that red wagon?" Harvey asked the group fishing for more information.

"I don't know, they didn't tell us anything about needing one." Travis said spoiling their fun and needling them a bit. He was curious himself but poor Harvey looked like he was going to have a conniption if he didn't find out more soon and he kept staring down towards the end of the docks to see if he could see anything that would give him a clue.

"Did they drive in? "Billy Lee said hopefully looking around the parking lot.

"I don't think so, they just walked up on us over here. I don't know where they came from." Molly said growing curious herself now not seeing any extra vehicles around. Last time she had saw them they had been driving the van, so if they walked over here that meant they must now be living close by and she would like to know about that. Not that she feared them in anyway, she just liked to keep tabs on who was likely to show up around her neighborhood unannounced and with them folks living so close by it would be awkward.

The group small talked and chit chatted for about 10 minutes with Billy Lee and Harvey hawk eying the dock every few minutes and posing questions until they announced Captain Vic, Frazer and Martha were heading back this way.

The story about Frazer and Martha having their differences with Molly and Bo had been out for a while with no one at the Marina really taking sides and saying it was a shame they couldn't get along. Most people were used to them avoiding each other and that was just the nature of things so the old couple coming back down here Captain Vic was pretty rare.

Vic started the explanation out by saying that he had just got done explaining to Frazier and his wife this new community meal and mutual aid society thing they were trying out and had been told Molly and Bo handled the catering on that. After saying that, Captain Vic just stepped back and let them have at it.

Frazier spoke first and advised he had no problem working with Molly and Bo if they had to on the details of the trade he had in mind but he wasn't in the mood for haggling and expected to make a profit someway. Molly said about the same thing back and they got down to the business at hand. It seems that Frazier in his attempt to snare a small alligator in one of his traps had had managed to catch a great big one and he didn't know what to do with so much meat except try to trade it here. Upon further explanation Frazier said that 11 foot or better gator was still alive and pretty feisty, well it was when they left the state park to come down here on their kick scooters a while ago anyway. They were using that mode of transportation daily now because they didn't have any gas for their van and it had taken them about an hour to make it here. They explained that they needed to go back and see about the condition of that snared gator before finalizing their deal but they didn't expect it could get away or that a bigger gator would come along to chomp it for dinner, because most gators don't get much bigger than that. That sucker was huge they reiterated.

Frasier original plan was trying to sell the gator tail to Captain Vic but they were going to need some additional help getting it down here as well as butchering it maybe.

"That's why I was asking about the wagon. You got to walk down a trail at the park to get to that pond I caught him in and I can't see any other way to move 8 foot of gator tail meat any other way except drag it out of

93

there with that wagon. I know you all got gas for sale up here, I just can't afford it. I was hoping to get enough gas up front to fill my van to bring that meat down here and have some left to ride around on." Frazier offered saying it would take him awhile, but him and Martha could do it all by themselves and manage just fine thank you, as Billie Lee and Harvey started circling them like buzzards and offering help for some commission or pay.

"I told him it was up to you Molly, I got no idea what two or three hundred pounds of that kind of meat would be worth." Captain Vic said thinking ordinarily he would just set a price on the gator tail and sell it to all the marina residents at a big cook out. A giant prehistoric sized one like Frazier was making this alligator tail sound like was quite a unique thing indeed to try to place a number on.

Molly thought for a moment and announced that she thought she could make jerky out of anything but she had never tried to do it with an alligator tail before as Tina reminded her that if their neighbor Joyce could salt cure eel she was sure she could do something with part of it so a deal started to get struck.

"Travis you need to get in on this deal!" Molly said motioning for him to come over to the picnic table where the discussion was being held.

"I don't need to be on that deal. I don't know what to do with all that alligator meat." Travis said backing off thinking it had nothing to do with swapping for paper goods.

"It's concerns part of you all's chicken and egg gas or cash money that I might be needing in order to cut a deal if that's alright. I know the community voted for your project and it's your right to say it stays dedicated only to that project but that sure is a lot of food they are offering that the community can use right now." Molly said eying his reaction skeptically.

"Why do I somehow get the feeling that this transaction is also going to cost me more hushpuppy mix?" Travis said with a smile indicating that he was up for a cook out, but he was unsure about that gas or cash contribution thing she was requesting as he took a seat.

They haggled and bantered for a bit until Molly explained she would like to make a special symbolic gesture of her own and offered 5 gallons of her own personal gas to Frazier and Martha and for trading purposes 5 gallons of gas and twenty-five dollars from the community fund that had already been contributed if Travis agreed. Ten gallons of gas was what the pair of stranded survivors had originally needed to leave town with to get to their friends in Alabama at the beginning of this societal break down and she then broke down and tearfully apologized to the old couple that she had once asked to leave her home and told them that they were welcome to come by her and Bo's house anytime they wanted to from now on. Martha gushed happily that this feud was over and gave both her and Bo a tear stained big hug as Frazier did the same saying "were friends again.". Everyone then calmed a bit and got back to business and sat back down misty eyed to plan a big community feast featuring fried gator tail nuggets and hushpuppies.

Harvey and Billie Lee were eventually volunteered or coerced to go back with Frazier to help kill the creature and fetch the gator tail back to the Marina. Bo and Travis said they would tag along and help fill up the vans gas tank while they watched the show of the men capturing the big pond monster.

"Are you sure you can shoot good enough to kill him first shot?" Harvey asked Frazier not wanting to be anywhere near a wounded gator.

"Oh, I have lots of experience shooting all kinds of alligators now I will have you know! There is a small area behind the eyes, that is about the size of a quarter. Hit that tiny bullseye, and the gator dies immediately. Shoot him anywhere else, and you're just asking for trouble, and lots of it. You also need to shoot sort of at an angle from behind and above the gator with the gun pointed roughly in the same direction that the gator's nose is pointing to be sure of what you doing. You boys don't worry about it, I shoot the small ones with a pellet rifle." Frazier said.

"He does you know! He said he ain't taking no chances with that one though and is going to use my 22. I told him shoot it with a slug out of that 20 gauge but he says he don't want to waste the shell." Martha said proud of her man's marksmanship.

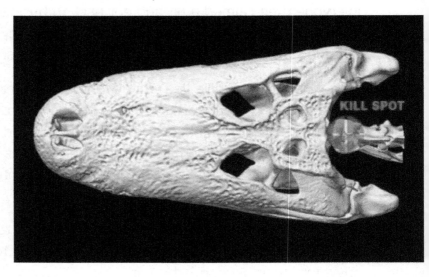

"How did you end up catching him? You said he is caught around his neck in a snare of some kind?" Travis asked wanting to know this trick.

"Ain't no trick to it, just think like a gator. I saw a duck nest the momma looked like she had abandoned and knew a gator would be sniffing around there before too long so I took me a stainless-steel coyote snare and some sticks and rigged me up a nasty little surprise for him. That gator is pissed off boys let me tell you! He is a regular tree shaker of a monster! I knew I had me a big one caught because I could hear him fighting that spring pole long before I even got close up enough to see what was in my trap." Frazier said describing how that big alligator got lured out of the pond and into the aircraft cable snare.

"Now then Molly, how do I get into this community chicken and egg community thing you got going on over here?" Frazier asked with a smile as they were walking to the vehicles.

5

The Reception Committee

Slim jumped out of the car door and checked the seventh or eighth mailbox for the day to see if they had any written response to the toilet paper-chicken egg barter/exchange scheme they were attempting. They hadn't seen any return notes or activity in most of the mailboxes that they had checked so far but one that was missing it's roll of necessity paper made them speculate and think about whether or not they should leave another roll if that person had not bothered to leave a thank you note or say something back to them. Spirits were still kind of high and they still had twenty miles or so of mailboxes to check before they got back to the fish camp. They retained their high hopes that somebody on this desolate stretch of road and small farms would take them up on their chicken egg barter deal either in this mailbox or the next.

The Reception Committee

As Slim walked up to the newest mailbox for inspection Steve called out to him that they had company coming and motioned towards a young kid about thirteen or so riding an old yellow Sting Ray bike with a banana seat carrying what was probably a BB or pellet gun. The kid had evidently come out of a driveway that might be the neighbors about a hundred yards up from where they were stopped at. He then proceeded cautiously down the road to within about fifty feet or so of them before stopping his bike and regarding them.

"Hey, we have been waiting on you!" The red-headed country boy exclaimed loudly.

"Why are you waiting on us? You need something?" Slim asked good naturedly holding up the new roll of toilet paper he had in his hand like he was Santa Clause or something stuffing stockings instead of mailboxes.

"We wanted to meet you to say that we will take you up on your deal if you have any more of that toilet paper available." The boy said dismounting his bike and slowly walking it towards them warily.

"If you got the eggs, then we got toilet paper!" Beth said exiting the car as Steve turned off the ignition and got out to stand by her.

"How many eggs for a roll of toilet paper are you asking?" the boy inquired shrewdly as he kept his bike between him and the strangers and held his pellet rifle with the best John Wayne style swagger he could muster.

The Reception Committee

"That's all going to depend on the size and color of the eggs that you are offering. Do you have Brown eggs or white eggs?" Beth asked.

"Or if they might be double yolks!" Slim quipped with a big smile and then introduced his party.

"We got both browns and white. My name is Jarred. I live about a mile or so from here and I was over visiting my neighbor discussing y'alls offer today and we decided to take you up on it. Are you wanting just eggs or you trying to trade for a stewpot chicken also?" Jarred asked warming up to the strangers after handshakes were exchanged all around.

"Now a chicken would be a wonderful and glorious thing to have. Your folks got any chickens to spare?" Slim asked watching as the young man glanced back over his shoulder at something.

"Could be. They are pretty pricey though and would probably cost you more than a month's worth of toilet paper to trade for a little scrawny one." Jarred said getting into his Huckleberry Fin country boy let's barter mode.

"Well, we wouldn't just want a scrawny one to eat, we would prefer to trade for prefer nice fat egg-layer if you know what I mean." Beth said, trying to negotiate a better deal.

"That would kind of defeat the purpose of me selling you eggs wouldn't it? I mean, if you don't want just a chicken today to eat and I swapped you for one of our prime laying hens, then I wouldn't have anything to trade with you tomorrow, would I?" Jarred said showing wisdom beyond his years.

"Well, you got a point there young son. I think what the lady means is that we would be more than willing to pay extra for a laying hen. We would rather have an egg tomorrow than eat a chicken today, if you know what I mean. You live too far from us to trade you for eggs daily. Of course, if you could find a way to do both and sell us some eggs and some laying hens we would be mighty beholden to you and your parents." Slim said regarding the boy.

"No offense, mister, but I ain't your son and I got me some of my own chickens at home that we are discussing here for trade. They are mine. I raised them by myself. You see me and a few other boys and girls around here raise some farms animals as Future Farmer Of America projects once in a great while and depending on what you want to trade for, you are going to have to satisfy me first." Jarred said before a voice called out from the woods across the road with an "Or me!"

A tall young man about fifteen or so with long shoulder length brown hair stepped out of the woods loosely holding a single-shot shotgun and evidently taking offense to his little brother apparently trying to hog all of the deal.

"Now who is this?" The startled Slim asked as Steve eyed the new young person warily.

The Reception Committee

"I'm his brother, Mark." The teenager said and then explained that fifty percent of that chicken flock that was being offered was his as well as his little brother's.

"No sense us starting to argue about the prices of who owns what chickens yet, let's just say we are going to trade for a chicken and get down to making some offers." Steve said smiling as Slim began warily eyeing the woods where their unexpected guest had just emerged from.

"Tell your friends to come join the parley." Slim said evidently spotting some movement in the shadows of the wood line.

"I told them boys to just sit there and hush!" Mark said disgustedly and then whistled for his friends to come join them.

"I bet he saw Stanley. That boy can't hide too good." Jarred said furrowing his brow as a group of three boys ranging in age from 11 to 14 sheepishly stepped out of the woods and walked onto the road.

"Ya'll wouldn't be setting us up for some kind of an apache ambush, would you?" Slim asked chuckling and looking at them with mock skepticism and indignance.

"No, not an ambush really, we are just being careful, mister. Can't be too careful these days, there are crazy folks about as you know. There's no telling who you will see out on this highway on any given day, but we knew you would be around sometime today cause of your note. We all discussed your arrival with our folks and they finally allowed us to try to talk to you about your deal, if you looked civilized enough." Mark said taking charge of his pellet and BB gun toting backup crew.

"This here is Dewey, Lester and Stanley." Mark said.

"Well, do you think we look civilized?" Beth said sort of mildly scolding the young boys before smiling.

"Oh, yes ma'am. You sure do. Didn't mean no offense to ya'll, we were just trying to be careful, like I said." Jarred spluttered before his elder brother took charge of the conversation again.

"Oh yeah, you all look just fine to us. Nice to meet you. We wouldn't have even showed ourselves to you at all if you looked dangerous or something. Thing is, our folks said if you wanted to do any trading, for us to be doing it at a distance and look you over real good first, if you know what I mean." Mark said regarding how close for comfort their parents thought they should allow the strangers to approach them.

"I can see the necessary caution in that. Your folks were wise to tell you that. Rest assured, all we want to do is exchange some of our paper products for some kind of food." Beth said regarding one of the younger looking in the face, but not much smaller physically than the older boys. Even though the world was in dire straits and people were starving everywhere, evidently this boy had not missed too many meals lately. He was the shy awkward pudgy type of a visiting cousin that was evidently the object of the other boys' ire and torment for being seen wearing his ridiculous Green Lantern comic character shirt in the woods and standing out as not cool or blending in at all compared to their camo or olive drab clothes and blue jeans –this boy was a sight! He had a semi-neon green shirt on with oversized almost white khaki shorts with colorful stitching on the back pockets that came down to his knees and was carrying of all things what looked to be a bright pink girl's Pumpmaster 760 Crossman pellet gun and a red school backpack. Why you probably couldn't hide that boy and his belly, let alone that stoplight red pack and those pants behind a whole forest of trees and with that pink pellet gun and neon green shirt you could probably still see him trying to hide somewhere over a half mile away!

"That's a pretty gun!" Beth said to which all the men and boys groaned at such a slight to their youthful exuberance and masculinity. The assembled youth of course, all started snickering as the boy called Stanley turned five shades of pink and red in embarrassment to match his pink rifle and began protesting loudly "THIS ISN'T REALLY MY GUN! IT'S JUST A LOANER AND THAT'S HOW I HAD GOTTEN STUCK CARRYING IT".

Jarred then commenced to telling them that Stanley had been sent to the neighbor's farm for two weeks of vacation before the grid went down and was supposed to be doing some sort of parental penitence or detention or something by removing him from his phone and game addictions of the big city. He was Lester and Dewey's cousin or some such. Dewey confirmed in his own youthful way that the boy didn't know jack about sneaking around in the woods not being seen or making much noise. The story of him being here at all seems that actually the uncle was a half-brother of the boy's father and the two quasi relatives were more like city lights in Vegas versus moss on an old oak tree when it came to living and kid raising arrangements.

"It's my BIRTHDAY today!" Stanley said with a little crack in his voice, trying to make a point of it that nobody was allowed to kid him about his appearance or lack of country boy ways today of all days.

"Well, Happy Birthday, Boy!" Slim said patting him on the shoulder enthusiastically.

"Happy Birthday!" Beth said and then on the spur of the moment decided to give the boy an embarrassing hug.

"I got to ask son, how did you end up with that pink pea shooter today? Was it a birthday present?" Steve asked with a wry grin that got loads of chuckles from the rest of the country kids.

"I told you it was a loaner! It belongs to Jarred and Mark's mom Silvia. Since I didn't have a pellet rifle she lent it to me." Stanley whined a bit miffed.

"Well, she lent it to you at first. But, then she gave it to you later on today, because it's your birthday! So, it's all yours now buddy, no living it down or saying it ain't yours from now on!" Jarred said with a laugh because it seemed to be one of the country boys' foremost favorite forms of entertainment these days to make that little chubby city slicker boy squeal or get his face to change colors like a chameleon, alternating between shades of blushing pink to boiling over lobster-red mad.

Slim rescued the besieged young man from anymore good-natured verbal abuse for a while by stating that he knew for a fact that the little pink rifle was the same model as the black pellet rifle he had proudly carried himself as a boy and reminded them what a fine weapon that was. Pink or not, it could still kill plenty of squirrels, rabbits, possums, rattlesnakes, whatever, you name it, it was a fine pellet/BB gun indeed no matter the color of its stock.

Stanley beamed proudly at the praise of the old man for his pink plinker and his compliment on its unique workings that made it stand out from other pellet guns, because it had that nifty five shot magazine the competition lacked. He was also pleased it was pointed out that it was plenty powerful enough to be hunting squirrels and rabbits and other critters with and did beseechingly ask them if they had any other color of paint that they might could contribute or trade him today. That exclamation caused lots of good natured laughter and more ribbing along with chuckled apologies that, "no they were sorry they didn't have any kind of paint with them, but they would bring him some back on their next trip to town". Funny that something as simple as house paint or any other kind of paint for that matter to get rid of that girly rifle color would have done so much for that boys' prestige and self-worth in this world, but paint now was somehow so hard to find.

"Back to the chicken eggs. I think two eggs for a roll of toilet paper is a fair price if it's a jumbo roll. But that gas station commercial stuff you left here last time you came through; my granny says it feels like sandpaper!" Jarred said rebuking them on the paper towel like qualities of the commercial toilet paper that had been left in their mailbox.

"Oh, we have some softer stuff for your granny if that's what she wants. But like that scrawny chicken for the stew pot ya'll offered us, it's got its price also. Now then, boys, what would you give me for this?" Slim said going to the back of the car and removing a giant roll of the commercial stuff made to fit a special wall container the size of a giant wheel of cheddar cheese.

The Reception Committee

"Holy hell! That's a hard thing to price!" Mark said looking at the giant roll of grayish thin abrasive commercial paper.

"Mister we don't have a toilet paper roll big enough for that thing to sit on so I say it's value is reduced and I don't want to be the kid that gets looked at like he traded the family savings for a pile of magic beans when I come to the house toting a roll of paper as big as Tubby's blond curly head over there." Jarred said poking malicious fun once again at Stanley, appropriate or not on his birthday.

"Well, everything has its value, I give you that and it's got its price, now for my way of thinking, it certainly beats using tree leaves or Spanish moss for the task of utilizing the outhouse and keeping the underwear clean. Now I bet you all if I am not mistaking, ya'll might have been most likely been reduced to pulling out some phone book pages or something to do that particular duty with before they had dropped off that last roll of toilet paper in your mailbox. So, which kind is better Jarred for you to want to trade for? Do you want more sheets of paper that lasts longer or do you want smaller rolls of softer paper that lasts a lot less time!" Slim said getting into his good 'ol country boy banter.

"Tell you what. Why don't you boys go get your parents to come meets us down there by the old white church at the crossroads in an hour or two and then we can all sit down together and see if we can do some trading." Steve suggested.

"That sounds good to me mister, but I am not so sure about our folks wanting to drive down there. I can hear them now saying there's the matter of the gas for them to get there with to consider, the fact that your strangers they don't know, and of course there is the all the safety concerns for our own homestead if they leave them unguarded I bet they want might want to keep in mind and consider. It took us two days just to convince them that we could meet you out here away from everybody to begin the negotiations!" Mark said.

"We could ride a bike that far to the church but it would take us an hour or so to get there and I am not studying how to ride a live chicken on my handlebars that far!" Jarred said contemplating having to go down there to do a trade.

"Well seeing how that it is Stanley's birthday and such, could you please tell your parents we got a bunch of fish fillets on ice from the coast we brought with us as well as some hush puppy mix and we could have us a church picnic fish fry and birthday party together!" Beth offered which drew quite a bit of excitement from the group.

"Dewey lives closest, I could ride my bike down to his house and tell his parents that before ya'll leave, but I'd just as soon negotiate with you here and now on that trade you offered. I got available two dozen assorted fresh laid eggs of my own stored in Styrofoam containers sitting over there on the edge of the woods and Dewey and them have 2 wicker baskets with a dozen eggs in each. I had them all ready just in case ya'll happened by like you said you were going to today. What would you give me for 4 dozen eggs?" Jarred said wanting to get back to bickering and bartering before the parents got involved or the trade grounds got shifted up the road.

"I think I could see my way clear to give you an eight pack of the good stuff. It has 2 bonus rolls in it that manufacture was doing as a promotion" Slim said studying the boy who appeared to be surprised by the first offer and deciding to go all in because there was nothing to be haggling about.

"Deal!" Jarred said as he rushed to the roadside to retrieve his hidden bounty as Slim went to open up the voluminous Cadillac's trunk and retrieve his trade goods.

"Now what are you going to do with it?" Mark said as Jarred was handed a gigantic pack of toilet paper that he had to figure out how to strap onto the sissy bar of his bike. Even though everybody had all kinds of bits and lengths of string, the task of securing it to the overgrown size of the sissy bar on that bicycle of Jared's wasn't happening.

Slim took that moment to teach all the boys a new useful and simple knot called the sheet bend. This is how you tie two lengths of rope or string of different sizes together and secure it with a knot.

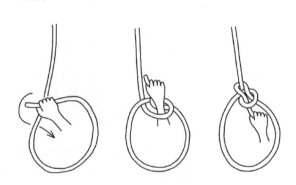

It seems useful knots are some forgotten lore once taught by Boy Scouts and ignored by millennials and the rest as one of the most useful skills a young man, young girl or a future sailor could know. The boys got sidetracked as Steve then demonstrated how to make a bowline. He explained to his avid listeners that this was one of the most important knots to know should you ever fall over a cliff or down a well or something in order to be hoisted out. His explanation included that to lift someone or an object up in the air where you did not want rope slipping or drawing it too tight was a lifesaver. He also demonstrated how you should be able to accomplish this task one-handed should you get your arm get broken in a fall or something.

Beth remembered how to tie this knot from her Girl Scout days the mnemonic "the rabbit comes out of the hole, goes around the tree and back in the hole" saying her way of remembering things helped the boys greatly in their efforts to reproduce Steve's efforts in teaching them this important life lesson.

So, shortly after one of the world's greatest knot tying parties and meeting of strangers concluded, jarred took off with his gigantic toilet paper bundle to go clue in Dewey's probably anxiously awaiting parents of the outcome of this meeting. It was about twenty minutes later when an old blue pickup truck with Jarred riding in the bed of it with his bike and a man that looked like Junior Samples off of the Hee Haw comedy TV show with the buzz haircut driving came back to their meeting point and he and his wife got out to meet the strangers.

It was uncanny how much the man resembled that lovable old backwoods country boy comedian Junior on the old Hee Haw show. It didn't help matters any that Dewey's last name was Samples either and that pudgy Stanley's girth didn't fall far from the family tree. The man's name was Marvis but he forever got branded as

113

Junior as a nickname in the assembled folks minds but not in their vocabulary around him.

"My name is Marvis Samples. I hear you want to trade for some of my boy's chickens!" Marvis began before Jarred squawked that his chickens had come first to barter for because he had talked to the strangers first.

"All in good time, boy. Thing is we appreciate ya'll stopping by all neighborly like and leaving us a message. Gave us a lot of hope seeing that silly roll of toilet paper. It is lucky we even found it. Why I quit looking in that mailbox almost half a year ago and I must say ya'll sure surprised us dropping off that necessity out of the blue. I tell you what, it sure did come on a good day. We had about used up all my scrap paper and the tax returns and we were getting close to using up all the pages in the books that we had on the shelves which weren't too many at all by the way and me and Granny got into a big row about whether or not the Lord would send me to hell for thinking about using a few pages of the family Bible! Now I don't recognize you folks from around here; where are ya'll from?" Marvis said putting his hands inside his bib overalls and causing Slim to eye him scrupulously to see if he had any concealed weapon riding on that lop of a belly he had.

"This family sure wasn't starving! Not by the look of them that was for sure. You can't cultivate that kind of lop over your belt in this apocalypse without eating regular and a lot. The big man had evidently lost some weight according to how his overalls were fitting loosely, but it

114

was hard to tell on these type folks physique anyway. But that they were eating something regular and a lot of it was fact and Slim took this as a miracle and it made him hopeful they might be willing to share and trade some of that surplus of whatever kind of food it was."

"I see you have met my boy and my little nephew over there already. My buddy Jarred here tells me that he managed to make a mighty fine trade with you already. I got to tell you though, it's dangerous times around here for you to stir up some shit that's liable to cause you a bunch of problems by being so public about messing with folk's mailboxes." Marvis said ominously.

"What do you mean? All we did was offer to trade some paper goods that we found and we were hunting for some chicken eggs." Beth said regarding the butch haircut heavy set man.

"Well not all neighbors talk to each other as you know. Not all people have the same opinion about others, you might say. It seems that you got everybody talking to each other around here anyways and amongst a bunch of country folks that don't particularly take to strangers that isn't always a good thing. Now I tell you what, I thought it was right smart about what you did to introduce yourselves but others may take it other ways, if you know what I mean. Some of them might not take it too good that you come on their property trespassing or that you are up to something sneaky by attempting to find out who around here might have any extra food. I wouldn't put it past some folks to think that you are just robbers trying to set us up to be honest so be careful." Marvis said scrutinizing them closely as Slim figured he did indeed have some sort of gun in his hand in back of them bib overalls.

"We didn't mean anything by the gesture. I can see now how our message might have worried some people but you got to start somewhere right? We had to be the first to pass the potatoes, if you know what I mean." Slim said making some obscure reference to passing the hot potato or problems around in the community.

"Oh, I had no problems with it at all. I thought it was right smart like I told you. But others got their own problems and sometimes they got their own dangerous or odd viewpoints. Meantime, Jared here says that you want us to have a birthday party for my nephew Stanley here at the old church. He said you had some ice cubes with you and I threatened to slap the boy for lying about that, but he said you seemed pretty trustworthy and swore it was true so here I am." Ol' Junior said sweating like a pig in heat and dobbing at his forehead with a big white hanky.

"Well, we don't have much ice. We got some big fish filets that we traded for down at the marina on the coast and as you know, a lot of those big fishing boats have ice makers onboard them so we got lucky. Now if you want a drink of ice water, we got that to spare! I wish we had some whiskey or lemonade to go in it, but like you said ice water is a mighty fine and rare thing these days itself." Slim said as he gestured Beth to get the large blue cooler out of the backseat and give them a taste with some of those darn little pointy paper Dixie cups they had tons of at the moment.

"Ambrosia! Sweeeet Ambrosia! Man, I didn't think I would ever see the day when a stranger just carrying me some ice water would be so welcome! Tell you what, ya'll come on down to the house and we'll talk further about this trading and birthday stuff ya'll been talking about happening later today and maybe we can have another cool drink with a little something in it if you don't mind under the shade of my porch!" Marvis said.

"What would you trade us for some fresh made hunters stew and greens and gravy? "Bessie May said just as rotund as her husband as she peered around him.

"Garden greens and gravy and we eat our fill? I have an eight pack of paper towels for your kitchen to soak up our leavings which I don't think there'll be none to wipe up when we get through!" Slim said exuberantly.

"Well, there ain't a whole lot but you will get a good meal that will stick to your ribs. The boys were supposed to be coming over also and having lunch with us considering we were allowing them to come out and meet you on the road as a posse of sorts for safety. But if you have time, I could throw in a couple extra handfuls of precious rice in the stew pot and you and your lady friend and I can get acquainted a bit more while making up some biscuits to sop the gravy with." Bessie May said regarding Beth.

The Reception Committee

"You have flour?" Beth asked in awe that such a rare commodity was being offered.

"I got that and some farm butter to go on them biscuits to boot! We still have us a milk cow in the shed that we share with the neighbors and we had plenty of flour on hand before the grid went down cause I used to make extra money baking cakes for the farmers market! I told Marvis here when we first got married and made him promise my PawPaw that we would always have besides a roof over our heads three things. Now if ya'll are city folks you won't appreciate this any but we have been living hand and mouth down here for generations both before and after the Great Depression, so these things matter to us. We always raised us a hog and a beef cow every year to feed the family. Now most say that was two things but I say it was one because it had to feed a family for a whole year. The second thing was he had to promise too, was that he always had to be good to me and good to our animals. That's another one of those doubled up things you might or might not understand. Then beyond all that, we had to have us a good garden with plenty of greens growing most of the year round. PawPaw always said if you had all those things, you wouldn't need to borrow money from an old man or be on the government dole and we would learn the wisdom in that philosophy eventually." Bessie May said with a hug towards her overstuffed man.

"Just because we are saying today that we have some extra food for you all that we will share doesn't mean that you are invited to the dinner table every day or that we normally have any extra food we don't need ourselves to be trading with you on a regular basis." Marvis cautioned.

"Oh, I understand totally, we don't mean to impose on anybody, you tell us if we get to sounding too pushy wanting to trade." Slim responded.

"Dewey, you ride with the strangers and show them where we live at. I got to ride up the road and tell Jared's folks the boy is o.k. and for them to come to the house for some supper if they have a mind to. You are going to have to put on your short eating bibs if they decide to come down because like I said, we are short on eatings and fixings today." Marvis cautioned and said that there would be a lot of water added to the stew today.

"We got all that fish we brought we brought with us, we can cook it at your place if you don't want to go down to the church and have a fish fry supper today." Steve offered.

"Why that's a fine idea, tell you what though. Bart is better set up than us for a fish fry because he still has gas for his outdoor fryer. Let's just go see what he says about having you all over and if it's alright Bessie May and I will tote over our food to share and we can talk more about this business of you wanting to do trading city goods for country ones." Marvis declared.

"That will be fine, do you want us to follow you or do you need some time to talk to him first.?" Slim asked familiar with the ways country folks did things.

"Oh, I think you better let me holler at him first. I am sure he is going to say it's alright, but he will have a bunch of questions about you all. You can hang out with Dewey and Lester at our house until I get back and then we can see about bringing our vittles over for the picnic party. I am going to take Stanley with me to ask him can we have his birthday party over there instead of having it at our place." Marvis said with a wink indicating there was a bit of adult subterfuge going on regarding celebrating the boy's special day.

"Ok, we will wait on you there then." Steve said looking over at Dewey who made a slight knowing face indicating he was in on whatever secret it was they had planned for Stanley's birthday.

"Stanley you can ride up in the front with us. Why don't you throw your gun and pack in Steve's car so it

120

doesn't slide around all over the truck bed?" Marvis said advising him there wasn't much room left in the cab with three large people riding in it.

"Dewey you and Lester take the laundry off the clothesline please when you get home. Just stick it in the basket and I will fold it later." Bessie May said.

"Ok Ma, we will take care of it no problem." Dewey responded and Beth knowing how young boys normally were when getting a new chore sprung on them was pleasantly surprised they hadn't whined a bit like most children that age sometimes do, but she just put it down to them having good manners.

"Tell our Dad we will be home in a little bit, we want to talk to the strangers a bit more." Jared advised as his brother Mark went to get his bike that he had hid in the bushes.

"Will do, you boys mind your Ps and Qs and don't give our company any trouble you hear?" Marvis warned before taking off in his truck as the group waved them goodbye.

"Mr. Steve you couldn't have come around at a better time! We have been puzzling over how to get rid of Stanley and distract him for a little while all day. You see we planned on having him a surprise party over at Jarred and Marks house anyway, but we got some preparations that need finishing before we go over there." Dewey said informing them that if they hadn't arrived when they did it would have been hard for them to pull off everything they had planned.

"So, you all were that sure we would come by today at this particular hour?" Slim said accusingly.

"No sirs, not at all. Well we counted on you coming by today, but we didn't know what time it was that you were going to be here. We got out here and hid in the woods early this morning and been sitting out here waiting on you for hours." Jarred said.

"So, you been hiding in the woods all day like a pack of wild Indians waiting for somebody to come by to scalp? I thought you said this wasn't an ambush? Steve said smiling.

"Well, it ain't, we just wanted to be first to greet you on your new mail trading route. You would have messed us up big time and we would have probably had us a very long wait or gone home if you had started in the opposite direction." Dewey said as his brother scrutinized him for some reason.

"Well you guessed right that we would be coming up from the beach, glad you didn't have to wait so long. Dewey do you think we got more people waiting on us up the road?" Slim asked noticing that strange look Lester had given his brother.

"Oh, you might, I don't think so though. Not many folks on this road raise chickens but our two families. Hey mister I hope you don't mind driving real slow in back of us, it's going to take us 10 minutes even pedaling at a good rate to get home or you can go ahead and meet us at that old run-down country store up the road. That place has been closed for years, but it's just up from my house." Dewey said.

"Well you all have too many bikes to put in the trunk so we don't mind just following you. Anybody else at your home?" Steve asked watching for their reactions.

"No, nobody else, that's why we need to get going if you don't mind. That and we got some chores to do really quick before my dad and Mom get back." Dewey offered.

"I heard taking the laundry in, what else you got to do?" Beth asked scrutinizing them also.

"They ain't leading you down the garden path or trying to deceive you or nothing. The chores refer to doing things for Stanley's surprise birthday party like bringing in the laundry. My old man taught them a neat trick so we can fix that boys clothes somewhat. I don't know what his parents were thinking sending him down to the farm dressed the way he does. That shirt he has on is the only green one he has and the rest of them look like a Hawaiian tourist convention. My Dad told Bessie May that green walnut hulls can be used to stain a white t-shirt so dark you can wear it when you squirrel hunt. She fixed up some of his clothes and hung them to dry so he doesn't stand out so much. Pop said in fact, back before all those different kinds of camouflaged shirts you can now buy at a sporting goods store, old timers he knew used walnut hulls to permanently dye their hunting shirts, which is what each shirt became after it was too worn to wear going to church back in the day." Mark said describing some of his prepper dad's country wisdom.

"Wow and I thought I was country, I never heard of that one before. We used to go to the Army Navy surplus store for hunting shirts." Slim said.

"You all sort of spoiled the fish fry for him, but not really. We had one planned already but he can wait until tomorrow to find out there's something else you can do with walnut hulls than die clothing with. You can take a washtub down to the crick and fill it with fresh water, then throw mashed up walnut hulls in a little eddy and watch sunfish and minnows of all kind come to the surface. Walnut hulls make it impossible to breathe underwater! If you grab them quick and put them in the fresh water tub they will recover and you can use them for trotline bait. But if there is a bass or a catfish or two in that little hole you dump your hulls into, you had better think about keeping them or if they are too small getting them upstream quickly or they will die on you. So will frogs and crawdads if they swimming around anywhere near." Mark said enlightening them to a neat cheating way of fishing and an extra use for that tub of die water sitting back at the house.

"Well I will be darned, you learn something new every day." Beth exclaimed.

"That boy is going to be pleased as punch later because we are finally going to be doing something about the color of that gawd awful gun of his, too. Not with walnuts though, Marvis had him a can of spray paint put back he was going to use on his smoker that we are going to use as one of Stanley's birthday presents to fix it with. I wanted to zebra stripe that rifle up and leave some pink on it so we could talk bad about him some more, but they won't let me do that!" Jared said laughing.

Rust-Oleum 248903 Automotive 12-Ounce High Heat 2000 Degree Spray Paint, Flat Black

"Now that would have been just plain mean, but funny!" Beth said smiling but seeing the country boy humor in it.

"Well if you did paint the gun that weird camo pink black, the deer and squirrels wouldn't see much difference anyway Deer sense colors toward the violet end of the spectrum, so they can see blues and probably even ultraviolet (UV) light. Deer show a slight sensitivity to yellow, but tests indicate that green, orange, and red appear to them as shades of gray. On the other hand, a squirrel's vision is unusually colorful compared to most animals, but by human standards, is still considered colorblind. Most squirrels have dichromatic vision, which means they can distinguish blue and yellow tones, but have red-green color blindness, like some humans do." Steve said.

"See I told you that just breaking up the pattern would help, I don't know what all them big words mean, but I was right!" Jared said before being told by Mark once more they were just going to paint it flat black and be done with it.

"So anyway, you see we need to get going so the paint will have time to dry before we give him back his BB gun" Dewey said and they made ready to leave.

All Stanley's presents had been hidden at the house and that boy didn't know how lucky he was to be even getting anything. Besides the very cool makeover his gear was getting there was also one small jar of jelly beans that they were going to give him as his very own. Everyone knew they were going to pester him to death to share such a delicacy with them but the gesture and meaning of the gift to do with as he liked was there. Bessie May had a penchant for buying bulk at the dollar store and breaking it down into what she called "Morale Builders" for times they were short on cash or couldn't get to town and this jar of jelly beans was the last of such delicacy's there was that had come out a huge bag of them.

She had read an article on Instructables that said to effect "Have you ever wanted to vacuum-seal leftovers to keep them fresh? Looking for a way to keep your popcorn or coffee beans fresh for longer? Want to vacuum pack dry goods for long term storage? If you answer "YES" but don't want to lay out $100 or more dollars for one of the commercial vacuum sealer machines, then do what I did - assemble your own for $30 from readily available parts! Using a $20 brake bleeder and a mason jar sealer, you can vacuum seal anything you can fit into a mason jar. "Bessie May said having taken that advice and went to town with it filling mason jars with everything from Beef jerky to M &Ms.

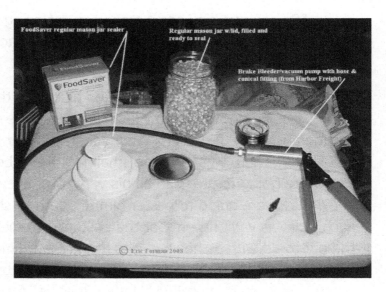

Getting Ready

Steve followed the boys past the old run down wooden general store that hadn't been open in years and pulled in the drive way and parked the car. The chickens were mostly free ranging roaming around the farm house's yard and the strangers were overwhelmed with this show of walking stock apocalyptic wealth. Chickens of all sizes, colors and breeds cluck-clucked there way here and there hunting for food as the occasional rooster made itself known with loud crowing.

"Dad said no talking about trading for live chickens until him and Mr. Bart, that's Jarred and Marks dad talks to you about it. You're lucky you even got this far in on the property because we usually don't let nobody past the gate." Dewey said.

"The old man usually has a shotgun pointing at you if you do. He saw you by the way sticking that roll of toilet paper in our mailbox." Lester informed them.

Getting Ready

"See I told you I had weird feelings filling up them mailboxes! I could have been shot! Slim griped.

"Well you weren't so be happy about that." Steve said kidding with him.

"How many danged chickens you got around here anyway?" Slim asked eying the strutting flock that seemed to be everywhere investigating the weeds for bugs or scratching in the dirt for little seeds.

"I dunno, maybe 40 or 50. We got more now than what we started with before the collapse if you can believe that. My pappy told me we were going in the poultry business and started raising them up just as soon as we heard the news about the electricity not coming on anymore. Hey have you all heard anymore about what's going on? The only radio station we get out here is the emergency broadcast system and they never say much of anything new." Dewey said as he and Lester got the walnut dyed clothes off the wash line and Mark and Jared saw about spray painting the pellet gun the best they could.

"No, we haven't got much news at all either. One of the boat owners at the marina has one of them big world band radios though and he listens all the time. He says folks are going to war in a lot of them little country's overseas but the U.S. is mostly staying out of it and trying to rebuild and keep the peace here. The big cities here like Chicago and L.A. are mostly toast. Our government don't say much about them but the Ham operators talk it up sometimes. There is no official statement on how many folks are dead around here but they estimate its over a 100 million." Steve said not sure he should be having this conversation with the kids without their parents being present.

"We got lots of dead folks on this road also. I am not sure how many but it's a bunch. Old folks were the first to go I know but we don't talk much to other families, too dangerous dad says. We also are not allowed to go around anybody's house we know has passed.' Jared said returning with Mark from their chore of freshly painting the gun stock and leaving it hanging from a piece of string from the rifle barrel.

"You sure got that done quick!" Beth declared.

"Wasn't nothing to it, but we were careful to do a good job." Mark said evidently having some previous skills at doing such a task.

"I still can't believe how many chickens you all got!" Slim said watching a mother hen usher her chicks about.

"It took some doing for us to build up the flock and we don't really have nothing to feed them with except some garden scraps and animal offal. Chickens ain't vegetarians like some city folks think don't you know." Lester said.

Getting Ready

"Well I guess they can find enough bugs and wild seeds and such on their own. Most of them look pretty healthy. Do you all still have a pig? I believe Marvis said something about raising one awhile back." Slim asked.

"No, we butchered him a long time ago and shared him out with Mark and Jared's family. We been meaning to go on a wild hog hunt and we know there is some around but here but we can't seem to find any yet. Do you know what tastes like pulled pork? A roasted possum! You ever ate a possum?" Dewey asked.

"Yea we have ate our share of them now but I will never forget the first two we tried. Our buddy Travis brought two back to fish camp from a hunting trip and we cooked them up. The first one tasted just like you said but the other one was terrible! "Beth said making a face about being pleasantly surprised by the first one and when she went back for more that second one tasted more like burnt plastic to her or something although they were both cooked in the same fire.

"Depends on what they been eating, best thing to do is catch them live and keep them in a cage and purge them. Either feed them some cracked corn or other grains until it's time to killem & grillem or if you ain't got that, give them some sweet wild plants or plantain and lots of clean water." Jared said knowingly.

Getting Ready

"We started doing that after Slim said the same thing but I still ain't over that skunk tasting possum." Beth said wearing a big "YUCK" look on her face.

"If a possum finds a dead skunk he would be liable to eat him. They ain't none too picky what they eat." Lester informed her.

"You think that's what happened? GROSS! Hey change the subject or I will never be able to eat one of those big rat looking things again!" Beth said with a shudder.

"We got something here that will make you forget all about that nasty taste. Hang on a minute and I will get whatever kind of birthday cake it is my mom made" Dewey said going inside to fetch it so they could bring it to the party.

"Oh yum! I wouldn't have known what kind of cake this was if she hadn't left her recipe card out. Its clabber cake!" Dewey said carrying a big sheet cake with white frosting out.

"What in the world is Clabber?" Beth asked.

"Clabber is a type of soured milk. It is produced by allowing unpasteurized milk to turn sour (ferment) at a specific humidity and temperature. Over time, the milk thickens or curdles into a yogurt-like substance with a strong, sour flavor." Dewey said.

Getting Ready

"That cake don't taste like clabber, it tastes like good old German Chocolate cake!" Lester said his eyes dancing in anticipation of eating some soon.

"Do you have any candles for it?" Beth asked

"No, we are out of candles." Dewey said sadly.

"WE got some!" Beth said going to the car to fetch some that they had scavenged from the restaurant supply truck. The consensus amongst the group was that lots of restaurants brought out a cake or a cupcake with a candle stuck in it a lot of times and this was the reason they were on that restaurant supply trailer and they had bunches of them!

"Wow mom will love you for supplying those! A birthday cake just ain't a birthday cake unless it has some candles." Dewey said.

Authors Note; In rural areas of the Southern United States, Clabber was commonly eaten for breakfast with brown sugar, nutmeg, cinnamon, or molasses added. Some people also eat it with fruit or black pepper and cream. Prior to the now-popular use of baking soda, clabber was used as a quick leavener in baking. It makes bread rise. Due to its stability, clabbered milk has been popular in areas without access to steady refrigeration

Getting Ready

"You think your mom would mind me looking at her recipe? That sounds so interesting and I want to see what else is in it!" Beth said.

"No, I will run back inside and get it for you, but when you are done reading it we need to get going if the paint is dry on that pellet gun." Dewey said and then run back to the house for the recipe card.

AUNT SUSAN'S CLABBER CAKE

1/2 lb. butter

2 c. sugar

2 eggs, beaten

3 1/2 c. cake flour

2 t. baking soda

3 1/3 T. cocoa

2 c. clabber milk

Cream together butter and sugar. Add eggs, one at a time.

Sift dry ingredients together and add alternately with clabber milk to creamed mixture. Bake in greased and floured 14x9-inch pan in preheated 350-degree oven 45 minutes.

Getting Ready

Measure carefully. (One-third tablespoon is 1 teaspoon.) A little too much cocoa makes the cake too dark, and too much flour produces a dry cake. How do you make clabber? Clabber is fresh milk that's soured or curdled. At this point, it's ready to use as clabber or to churn for buttermilk. You can substitute buttermilk in this cake

How to make clabber

Farm fresh raw milk (unpasteurized), about a week or two old is best.

Process:

Leave your milk on the counter in a jar (sealed) for 2-3 days in a warm spot until solids appear. Shake it to see if it's turned thick. It should not yet be separated.

If the milk is still mostly white when shaken, and has turned thick, it is done clabbering. Store your clabbered milk in the refrigerator. If you leave the milk on the counter longer, it will separate turn into curds and whey. If this happens, drain off they whey and cream cheese and use in your favorite recipes.

Party Down

Jarred and his brother took off on their bicycles heading for home about 10 minutes away before Dewey and his brother squeezed in with Slim in the back seat of the Cadillac with the cake on Dewey's lap for safe keeping.

After introductions were made to Bart and his Wife Silvia it was soon birthday boy time! The strangers all laughed and enjoyed being a part of the elaborate hoax to give the kid a surprise party that they had somehow become a major part of. That was one happy young man and one humdinger of a birthday party let me tell you!

It seems the tradition around here for such affairs is presents first, then cake, then birthday dinner, all followed in short order with the kids going off one way and the adults going the other as soon as the dishes hit the sink after the kids carried them in.

"Here have a slug of this." Marvis said producing a stoneware jug.

"What is it?" Slim asked grinning as Marvis wafted the cork in front of his nose.

"An alcoholic beverage that will make you walk side-ways, and make the ugliest girls look pretty!" Marvis said with a loud hoot.

"Oh hell! You boys play nice and you warn them folks about that white liquor you all brewed up. That stuff can set your brain on fire. Pour me a shot there, would you Marvis?" Silvia said as Bart passed her one.

Stanley had run off to whoop it up with the other boys for awhile sporting his new hunting clothes and joyfully toting his non-pink pellet gun. After learning the wisdom behind how they had dyed his clothes it was immediately decided that they all should go over and dunk that red school bag pack looking thing of his in that walnut wash and see if it took. It was sort of undecided how that waterproof nylon and the zippers was going to react to the dye but Marvis assured them Walnut hulls are used to dye steel traps so it should work just fine. He advised that you can also dye your modern cable snares if you want to with it but to be advised the aluminum ferrules will not take the dye

"Wear gloves or you will dye your hands! Now depending on what color you want to end up with remember that the softer outer hull of Black Walnuts is what you use for dye. When they are green, they will give you a weird off greenish dark color. When they are dry or blackish looking, they will give you brown. You can go from light to dark by the concentration of hulls and time you immerse something in your mix. The inner hull is almost useless for dye. You need to "Shuck" the walnut shells and same the outer shell. You can store them in a sack for years by hanging them up in a dry place. Some People used to boil their traps for hours in river water (NO CITY CHLORINE) to get the preservatives out of the metal. Then they would dry them so that the dye would take better. A lot of folks just boiled their traps to get the grease off and let a film of rust start to form. Some people swear by melted paraffin in a kettle of boiling water and slowly dipping them and retrieving the trap from the pot. The floating paraffin was supposed to rust proof the trap I heard but I have had mixed results with this. Now be sure not to wax your body grips (Conibears), it makes them too "unstable". You can use speed-dip, paint them, or dye & omit the wax process. If you are using them on land sets, treat them early enough to allow them a few weeks to "air-out". If they are for watersets.....they're good to go once dry, as the animals can't smell underwater." Bart said sharing a bit of trapping knowledge.

"Bart we might have to disagree here and I will tell you why after I give everyone another sip. I once had a me a pet Coon and a dog that would readily smell out and locate submerged fried chicken bones. Dangdest thing you ever seen. Dogs as you know are now trained and used to find submerged drowning victims. Now when you think about it that way, you got to take into account that many people swear that they can smell bedding Bluegills and Shellcrackers. That all kind of It makes me believe that some smells will come to the surface." Marvis said who had learned a few different ways or traditions of trapping.

"Well Marvis there might be something to that. When I made that statement about animals not being able to smell underwater, I was pretty much talking about an animal that was swimming underwater. Rats, coon, mink, etc. seem to be either less sensitive, or they are somehow less concerned (and I am saying this only as a kind of a "generalized" statement) with odors with them critters....than say with K9's (coyote & fox)." Bart responded.

"Tell our new friends all about anglers smelling bedding fish, I bet they never heard that before. It was so nice of you all to bring that fine saltwater fish up here! Thanks again! But I tell you what, those two men sitting over there used to be some fishing fools for bluegills before they needed to stay at home and guard the houses. We have had many a fish fry off of them going off to the river or lake and carrying back 50 or 60 of them tasty panfish." Bessie May said beaming her approval towards her husband and Bart.

"I can smell a bream spawning bed as can many other bream fishermen. It's just a talent you get taught growing up. The bed will generally smell like overripe watermelons some folks say, to me they just smell like fish. Now if I am searching for new spawning beds I'm going to look for downed trees in 2 to 5 feet of water and look for foamy bubbles. When the bucks (*bucks and hens are how they refer to males and females*) are fanning the beds, they churn up a lot of bubbles, and sometimes you can smell them and sometimes you can see a little scum on the water." Marvis said before Bart started sharing some of his own fishing expertise.

"Now me. I start by looking for shallow flats or long sloping banks where the fish are likely to spawn. Now I have seen other fishermen find spawning bream many ways. Sometimes they claim you can see their fins or the swirls they make. Some folks use their ears and listen for smacking sounds made by fish sucking bugs from the surface or beneath lily pads. My way is different. I use my nose now that Marvis taught me the trick. Wherever bluegill nests are concentrated, the air carries a distinctive fishy odor. Anyone with a normal sense of smell can learn to zero in on that musty aroma and find big beds holding scores of good-eating panfish." Bart said acknowledging his mentor.

"Now I ain't the only one that shared a secret or two to catching a bunch of bluegill, Bart here taught me the key to finding likely locations to sniff around at is finding shell beds where bluegills nest. Take a cane pole with you, go toward the middle of a cove or a slough, and use the pole's butt to poke the lake bottom. When you feel something crunchy and hard, that's a shell bed. Fish there and you going to fill up your stringer. You will often see piles of small, white snail shells littering the bottom, sometimes mussels but where there are shells there is bluegill.'" Marvis responded.

Meeting A Prepper

"So, Bart, Marvis and the boys told me that you were some kind of a prepper. I have some good friends of ours that are moving from our fish camp to the beach that followed that worldwide preparedness movement and logic before the grid went down. All their prior planning seems to be paying off now and has helped them a lot now having a few things they needed available." Steve said referring to Tina and Travis.

"You can call me a Farmsteader, Homesteader, prepper, country boy survivalist it's about all the same to me. I used to identify and call myself a prepper. I just say I was more prepared for this crap to hit than most now. How about you all? Did you ever dabble in the survivalist mentality or put up preps for a disaster like this?" Bart said appraising their facial reactions.

"Us? No not really Bart, we had plenty of reason to be viewed as such or become one though over the years.

You forget that we lived through the cold war years etc. and everyone back then including the school system learned a bit about civil defense and disaster preparedness as just something you needed to be aware of and teach. Now us personally, we never went all out personally for stockpiling extra food or anything for a nuclear disaster, we had friends that did that and we had friends that spent a lot more money doing same thing getting ready for Y2k and such. Glad nobody ever needed any of that end of the world stuff they bought but we found it kind of obsessive and didn't go in for it. However, don't get me wrong we always knew to keep extra food for snow storms or job loss etc. in the house and we ending up getting a week or two extra like during the Cuban Missile crisis." Steve said not really liking the label of a prepper or survivalist just because they usually kept a full pantry for hard times or bad weather like their parents and grandparents had.

"Well survivalist, prepper whatever label people tend to use these days to describe emergency preparedness you will find that they are the ones usually that end up thinking of spending a lot of money on a lot of costly preps but that's not the true definition of survival by any means. Comparability, that's the key and the word I use to describe my prepping and thinking now. Why I was a dang fool like all of us newbie preppers starting out focusing on reading the preparedness forums, joining the movement and breathlessly watching the gear and gun vids. Then I thought why? I am poor as a church mouse and can't afford all that crap and could probably outlive most the people that were rich enough to have it. It seems that everyone at first is thinking the only way they will survive is if they somehow manage to buy a this or that bit of prepper gear and they all end up spending way too much money for way too much bullshit other than long-term storage food. I finally realized after I wised up myself after a few years that I already had most of what I needed to just plain survive with from being in the Boy scouts when I was a kid. That was when I and a whole lot of other kids I grew up with had no problems at all with getting by in the woods and depending on a lot of basic woodlore knowledge that we took for granted and only depending on a little bit of gear to have a goodtime, camp and hunt and fish well." Bart said.

"Yea back in the day the Boy Scouts used to get even the inner-city kids to get out and spend some time in the woods learning some basic campfire skills. I doubt that you will find very many people these days from the last couple generations that could build a brush shelter or make a fort like we used to do just for entertainment purposes as boys growing up." Slim said.

"I also learned a lot about life from the way my daddy and momma used to turn me out of the house to go play and wander the woods and fields and be free learning nature. Why kids were left dang near on our own to do it most of the time. We didn't have no whoosey what's it apps on a cell phone to identify plants with or have it on us at all times to be used to let mommy and daddy track our where abouts and communications with. I

144

compare what I need to survive today like it was a boy scout camping trip and reduce it down to the basic elements and minimalist gear I need for the length of the stay or he time in the woods to accomplish a task. More folks in the prepper community I think should do the same. I have studied many ways of survival in military schools as well as life and spent way too much time doing extensive research on the internet on primitive and modern-day survival and I haven't really ever seen the advice distilled down to only one thing other than lots of ranting and raving on why you need various types of firepower or so-called survival guns. You know what the best survival gun is and the best knowledge and skills to have for an apocalypse like this all boils down too? A damn country smart 13-year-old kid with a pellet/BB gun. Throw one of them farm boys out in the woods in his back five or forty acres that he normally roams around on every day and you got a survivor. Put an Army Ranger with an AR 15 with his military issue ammo on that same strip of land and see who is going to be eating well and surviving better in a week or two all by their lonesome. The kid that knows the lay of the land, nature and the animal's habits in his area along with all the wood craft knowledge his Uncles and his cousins taught him over the years and he is going to surpass and out match that elite military soldier's skills hands down. There is no doubt about it, he knows where the best place to hunt squirrels or go fish at as well as the best places to hide from his little country buddies up the road dirt clod war games when they play." Bart said with a chuckle thinking about how he had his two boys out stomping the woods and toting a Red Ryder BB gun as quick as he could." Bart said and was encouraged to talk more about his philosophies by his attentive and appreciative audience.

"Well back to the survival gun issue. I studied the air gun classics that are still around today like I grew up with, the daisy 880, Crossman 760 pump master etc. and I came to a conclusion about that prepper mnemonic "two is one and one is none" saying the preparedness forums like to throw out as the ultimate wisdom and excuse we use to justify for our duplicated prepping expenditures as kind of waste if you didn't look at buying just what you need preps correctly to begin with. You got to look at first why am I buying this thing and what it is for and then compare cost and carry weight to get the same job done. People want to buy a regular .22 caliber hunting rifle for many reasons, they are affordable, ammo is cheap (or was) they are dependable, they are perfect for small game etc. and I then think hey a cheap quality kids pellet rifle/ bb gun can do all that and do it cheaper and have they have several advantages all their own. The biggest positive advantage being that you can shoot an air rifle in your backyard most places, you can't do that with a 22 rifle and an air gun is a lot quieter. A big mistake a prepper makes often times when it comes to purchasing their first air gun is lack of research and hands on experience with the product. They are usually already mentally wearing out by now with regular gun facts are well-versed studying for instance 45 pistol or 9mm, who makes the best AR, choosing a

Mossberg 500 shotgun or Remington 870 etc. and comparing various bullet and shot ballistics so what can go wrong they figure, it's just a pellet gun they are considering for hunting small game usually. It doesn't take the uninitiated new air gunner very long to find out that not everything they knew about pellet guns was wrong, just most of what they based their first purchase on. Take for example when you are looking at the latest, greatest newest crop of lightning-fast (up to 1500 fps) .177-calibers at your local big-box store. Got to be some kind of crazy-good, faster is always better right? You want one of those right? You want one that has pretty wood stock like a real rifle correct? Nope Wrong. Most of them newfangled air guns are lousy—hard to cock, loud, often very heavy and some the absolute hardest guns to shoot accurately it seems. That's not my opinion by the way, that is the opinion of noted authority and air-gun designer Tom Gaylord He is a 50-year enthusiast of the sport and a well followed blogger with PyramydAir.com, a source for all things air-gunny. One of my favorite Gaylord explanations of this phenomena is air guns operate in a parallel universe to other guns. And very different rules apply. Now my comparable prepper takes on this is that for less than the cost of one of most those super-fast pellet guns I am probably going to be disappointed with. I can if I want to or choose to, have two of the cheaper time tested and durable (yea they are plastic but they last the rigors of youth) but powerful enough to get the job done ones that I am used to. These pellet guns are comparably much lighter, can shoot BBs or Pellets (expensive pellet guns are one shot pellet only usually) the cheap ones are super easy to pump, accurate and surprisingly powerful enough for small game hunting at shorter distances. No brainer right? Plus, I have money left over to buy a years' worth of ammo and other stuff. I love having the capability to use BB, s on small birds in a survival situation. I can think of all kinds of things to cook from my garden or with beans and rice that the addition of little bits of chopped up meat go well with and I ain't above cheating and shooting them over sprinkled birdseed which is also cheap and baiting a field. So, add to my initial purchase some bird bait if you will like sunflower seeds etc. to increase my chances and assure me tasty targets.

"That wasn't a classic Daisy or a Crossman that I see Jarred carrying, what brand is it?" Slim asked thoroughly familiar with the looks of the old two standby beloved pellet guns he had grown up with.

"That my friend is the Umarex APX! Those pellet/BB rifles in my opinion are is the most outstanding and affordable survival tool that has come along in a long time. The company engineers had fun with that project it seems and have taken modern technology and older classic designs to the pinnacle point of affordable preparedness and young adult small game hunting. My kids got upgrades to their basic bb guns but not like they expected. See times and money were tight and I advised them this Xmas that me and mommy were watching our pennies this year and that they wouldn't be seeing any wooden stock pellet rifles for some time because the big footed growing critters called boys needed new shoes and socks, winter coats and other stuff but I managed to put a bit of overtime in at work and come up with the all-time best upgrades they would see for a while for their old well-used pellet guns which was a daisy red Rider for Jared and a Daisy 880 for Mark. I got them both Umarex APX rifles that seem to be in some way permanently attached to their hands ever sense. Hardly a day went by when school was out that they weren't carrying them downstairs from their bedroom and leaning them in the corner over there until they got done with breakfast and then they were back in hand heading out the door until it was time to come in for lunch." Bart said.

Bonus Author Insights On Budgets And Prepping

Everything gets reduced to just "what if" in some preppers minds, just "if" we had better equipment we would be able to survive longer and easier maybe. So, we often times we go over budget and buy more crap and by buying the same dang thing because it looks cooler by being camouflaged now or something we forget that the same non-tactical looking thing that we already have on hand can do the same job or better if we just practiced with it more instead of buying some new and improved shit that sounds good for the time it takes to pull our credit card out and get it.

The need and necessity of such a gesture always seems to be hurried up by our desire to get it in our hot little hands before the crap hits the fan and the endorphins in our survivalist mindset override our common sense and financial where withal to make more sound judgements. But that's what we do and get a rush like that prepper goods mail or ups delivered to our doorstep high we get from thinking we are solving the survival problems of the world with this next shipment. Our justifications are many our wallets are empty! money pits and there ain't one better way to lose money quick than prepping without a clue or listening to bad advice. Really, we are our own worst enemies in many ways when it comes to such because we all know in our heart of hearts that somehow in our fantasies we are going to miraculously use our own survival mindset to "remember or repurpose a piece of gear we have personally added to our preps that everyone in our forums will hold us in awe for thinking of or the alleged experts have seemingly so far overlooked." Its, fun, its enlightening, its challenging and one of the best outcomes of it is individual confidence building as we progress in our knowledge, but it's expensive. Boy is it expensive, but to a prepper often worth it. Be honest with yourself and if you think about our most not thought out decisions or worst investments, they can usually be found to have something to do with prepping if your deep into that. But I digress!

.

9

Air Guns And Attitudes

You know if I had any sense and extra cash before this disaster happened I would have been looking for bb guns at yard sales before the poo hit the fan and been putting them back. That's hind sight now but think about it, if a neighbor came by asking for food I could have handed him or her a so called no longer wanted kids toy with some pellets and bb's and give them probably their one and only chance to feed themselves. Such simple pure logic, such wishful hindsight now could have lowered their fears, increased their morale, poise a relatively small risk for me (much better than lending a 22) and I doubt if I told them I didn't want them coming back around they probably wouldn't have except for maybe to beg me for some more cheap pellet or BB ammo for it that I can buy cheaply and store easily while the grid is up. Those powerful and inexpensive air guns directed to youth sales are a real game changer when you apply prepper logic to

151

them let me tell you!" Bart said applying his unique prepper sense to trying to solve the "starving neighbor" problem.

"So what kind of an air Rifle do you have stashed around here for yourself Bart? I know you have one around here somewhere as enthusiastic about them as you are." Slim said.

"Me? I am very proud to say I got two! But the boys are constantly borrowing my main squirrel gun which is my Umarex Forge so I guess I will have to talk about my other one first. It is what I call me my Homefront hen house gun. Now I am sure you know somebody always needs to stay home to guard the chicken coop and the preps these days and that's usually me. Now every two legged or four-legged critter in the woods has an appetite for birds and eggs and wants access to the chickens so they need to be guarded closely. The animal varmints that might want an egg or a chicken for dinner can easily become my family's supper from a distance with this extremely accurate rifle. I got it topped off with a sweet variable 2x to 7x scope made by one of Umarex's subsidiaries called Axeon that is crisp and exactly what I need in capabilities for hunting or target shooting." Bart said showing off a very unique looking PCP (Pre-Charged Pneumatic) air rifle.

"That fine critter getter is called a Umarex Gauntlet, I wanted me an air rifle that I could target shoot with as well as use for a ground blind turkey hunting rifle. I ain't real good at calling gobblers in close so I needed me something that I could get enough practice shots off at the range with to get real accurate and do it without me having to constantly pump or cock a rifle to death. I chose that model also because I am a firm believer in quick follow up shots. You need this capability particularly when it comes to predators around chicken coops. Sometimes animals get hungry all at once and you can have a group of critters like raccoons or coyotes come to visit or be trying to aim at an egg robber like a snake that can duck, dodge and slither real fast into cover. I tell you what, chicken house guarding is usually boring and a pain in the ass most of the time but occasionally it is like hunting on a baited station from my bedroom window. "Bart said with a loud guffaw explaining he could rain 10 pellets of lead towards the hen house and reload for 10 more in seconds if need be.

"He can easily bust a turkey in the noggin at 65 yards plus." Jarred said proudly beaming his approval and hero worship of his Pops hunting and shooting capabilities.

"Wow that is some fine shooting! That rifle must be wicked accurate! I ain't to good at getting one of them bearded easily spooked birds to come to me neither. I bet with the rifle and scope set up you can really play Ma Bell and reach out and touch someone! Can I see it? That sure is a big gun Bart, how many feet per second and how many shots do you get out of it?" Steve said reaching for the gun and then exclaiming that it "wasn't bad weight wise at all and felt good to him."

"Actually, I know for a fact that I can shoot accurately a lot farther than that with it. I get 60 shots at a consistent 900 FPS in .22 caliber from a tank fill. That's the cool thing about that gun, I got a bicycle pump looking affair to refill it with but that pump is far stouter than one of those you use on a bicycle. A regular bicycle pump won't fill it, they can't get up to pressure that is needed. The rifle weighs about eight and half pounds, I admit it looks a bit bulky at first to the uninitiated but even a Ruger 10/22 carbine would look bulky if you strapped a can of Raid bug spray under the barrel." Bart said chuckling about his comparison to the rifles 3000 psi high capacity regulated HPA tank.

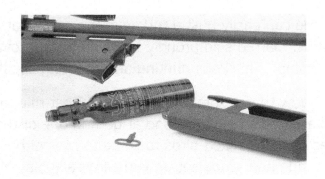

"Wow That thing is stout! Feels about as strong and heavy a solid piece of heavy steel pipe. I wasn't expecting that at all! That is a powerful well-made pump my friend!" Steve said weighing the pump in his hand.

"Yea they are kind of pricy but you have to pay for that kind of machined precision and durability." Bart said

"What is that thing attached to the pump?" Steve asked.

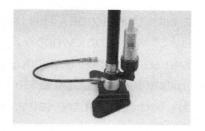

"That is the Dry Pac attachment that installs to the base of the pump and functions as a scrubber to remove water from the air that is to be compressed. The Dry Pac removes 90% of the moisture from the air to keep your tank and pump as free from water as possible." Bart advised

"You got that right! I can see how it is a good target rifle with that adjustable cheek piece feature and it dang sure weighs far less than one of those expensive techno looking Anschutz .22 caliber single shot Olympic match rifles. This nice rifle is actually comfortable to carry, I like the curved forearm. It just feels right." Steve said before whistling appreciatively as he pointed the fog and shockproof nitrogen gas filled scope out the window towards the chicken coop and appreciating the sights clarity.

"Let me try that a minute." Slim said reaching for the farmstead weapon and then shared the same appreciative oohs and ahs Steve had said along with how ergonomic and flowing it was to do quick sweeping follow up shots with. He then cranked the scope up to seven power and did a sweep of the poultry yard and made a face as he handed the gun back to Bart.

"Something wrong with that scope? The higher power of it limits your field of view somewhat but that's to be expected, or did you see something suspicious over there?" Bart said as he quickly looked out the kitchen door towards his unguarded chicken coop at the far end of the yard suspiciously.

"Dang he wished he had a farm dog or even a barn cat around this place." He thought. He had both of course before the grid went down but the adopted Humane Shelter rescue dog that his wife always said looked suspiciously like a wolverine he had feel in love with upon seeing was old when they had got him and five years of running wild every day with a pack of boys and trying to keep them out of trouble and guard the chicken house against all kinds of critters had did the old pooch gentleman the kids had lovingly called "Mutt Mutt" in. It hadn't helped that the old dogs failing heart much that he had been reduced to eating meager table scraps during the hard times along with the occasional people vitamin pill slipped to him on the sly by Bart, a practice his wife disapproved of as an empty bottle on the shelf still remained as a constant reminder to her of their now nonexistent supply of them. The old dog had just laid down, gave up and died one evening and "cat" had disappeared mysteriously shortly thereafter. The cat was there one minute and like cats do sometimes simply wasn't there the next.

"Oh, I know all about scope field of views and adjusting the focus of the cross hairs for the operators own personal eyes. I just saw something a second ago closer than I wanted to see." Slim said somewhat embarrassedly because he was in mixed company explaining that the big leghorn rooster of Bart's had taken an inopportune moment in his opinion to fill up his crosshairs with something best left unsaid while mounting a hen and that wasn't a sight he cared to see so close up ever again.

Hoots of laughter of the assembled party occurred as Slim turned 20 shades of red in humiliation as the boys giggled immaturely but fully familiar with farmyard animal husbandry and Slims discomfort at various snide remarks.

"You boys go on outside and tend to your chores" Silvia said directing the little grinning mischievous heathens out the door with an admonishing "mind their manners look "or they would get a talking too about treating their elders and household guests better later.

The rest of the guys were still sitting around grinning a bit about how Slim had taken viewing a chicken getting him some at seven power and the uniquely aggravating and embarrassing boyish remarks that had come from the youngsters in Slims direction which had caused Silvia to give them the Momma bears famous "mind your manners" look any sane man soon realizes means "We don't discuss such in this house" and fumbled around to change the conversation.

"They got any gas available for sale down on the beach?" Bart said pointedly as his wife appeared to pay close attention to this new tact in the conversation.

"Yes, there is some gas available there, but it's a pretty pricy and scarce commodity to get ahold of as you can well imagine. From what I have heard and seen so far there still are several unscrupulous folks that would try to charge you a hundred dollars a gallon for it if they knew you had that much money in your pocket However, from what I have seen so far, I would have to say that the Marina has the right handle on what is a fair price or what is considered free trade pricing per gallon that's open for negotiation. See them big gas guzzling boats docked over there have huge fuel tanks on them designed for long pleasure or leisure trips and those ones specifically designed for deep sea commercial fishing have sometimes even bigger ones. center. Since neither one of those activities makes much sense anymore all of the leisure craft, yachts, charter fishing boats and the big long liners stay in port and the captains and crews pretty much mostly beach or dock fish for themselves unless a community effort is going on. They marina residents mostly all live on the water so going out deep sea fishing or otherwise just don't make sense and they need to conserve fuel for when they might need gas to get to a safe port if a hurricane, fire or any more social unrest happens. They use the wharf for trading and the boat is just their abode. A parked boat is prime retail real estate these days if you can protect your dock space and they have come together to make it a safe place for those that come by looking for help or searching for supplies they want to barter for." Steve's wife Beth said

Bart had retrieved his favorite squirrel gun from his son Mark and handed it to Slim for inspection.

"Beautiful..." Slim murmured admiring it.

"Tell me something more about it." Slim said admiring it before passing it over to Steve for his inspection.

"That my friends is another fine Umarex rifle called the Forge. We are a Umarex family if you haven't figured that out by now. You can't beat them for technological advanced consistency in power, value and price. They stand behind their stuff also, Umarex really rates as a company with me by offering a 3-year warranty on their air rifles. This, of course, is 3 x greater than that provided with most air rifles in this price range. It gives a sense of security to the owner and confidence that he/she has made a good long-term decision. I was all set up to buy my wife a Umarex of her own when the power went out, talk about bad timing and bad luck! Anyway, mine is a little big and heavy for her because she is a small woman but she shoots it. The cocking effort is very low for an air rifle of this power level. The specifications on that one is it's a .177 Gas-piston and with a single pump, this air gun can send a lead pellet down range a smoking 1050 foot per second and with an alloy pellet you get 1250 FPS! It's a lot easier to cock than a lot of break barrels at 30lbs which is a feature that I really like and my wife appreciates. Check out the fit and finish on it! Very tight and fine lines. Notice how the mechanism meets the stock. That is a wonderful feature called the Nucleus Integrated Rail Platform which encases the TNT (Turbo Nitrogen Technology) gas piston chamber. This long Picatinny rail is *forged* with the action to reduce noise, vibration, and to maintain your scope's zero.

"You got any tips or tricks for hunting squirrels that you want to share with us? Steve asked eager to hear some of the man's hunting wisdom.

"That all depends on how you like to hunt them and the terrain they are in. Some squirrel hunters prefer to stalk hunt through the woods. If you doing that I would try carefully walking through the forest floor after rain has made the leaves less crisp is a very effective method. So is finding a spot to sit and wait for squirrels. Now the first thing you got to do is find a squirrel. The best way to locate squirrels is to scout and search out their feeding areas. You need to look carefully for nut-bearing trees such as oak, hickory or walnut. Look at the forest floor, cracked shells on the ground are a good clue that squirrels have been there and will return. At daylight or the hour before darkness, I pretty much find me a comfortable spot to sit and wait in a known area. Now for those who stalk squirrels like my boys they usually find a little more action. Those squirrels usually see the hunters before the hunters see them. Thus, a battle of wits begins with a wild squirrel that has survived attacks by hawks and owls from the air and coyotes and foxes on the ground, at first, he seems to hold the edge. The squirrel typically runs up a tree and will try to position itself on the side of the tree opposite the hunter. That's when it's good to have a hunting partner around, a squirrel hunting dog is better than a human for this task but another hunter you are familiar with works good also. A hunter on both sides of the tree usually triggers a race highlighted by tree-to-tree jumps by Mr. escaping Squirrel." Bart said

"I agree, the best time for me is to hunt gray squirrels is early morning, though the last hour of daylight also is good. They'll be more active all day on cloudy days. Well into the early fall, you can go out in the woods early in the morning and find squirrels with your ears. Just listen for the sound of squirrel teeth gnawing away on a hickory nut." Marvis said exhibiting some of that wily wood wisdom of his.

"It didn't take me long growing up to find out that the gray squirrel in the back yard and the gray squirrel in forests are the same but different in many ways. Suburban squirrels are accustomed to people. Squirrels in the wild are wary of humans. Hunting them takes some skill but you can increase your odds with a trick or two. Marvis can call them in with his mouth or using a commercially made squirrel call. I never got the nack to do either of those things well but my daddy taught me a good trick that works. Squirrels can be called in by rubbing two quarters together. The edges of quarters are etched, so when you rub one edge against the other it sounds something like a squirrel chattering." Bessie May said.

"Now I am going to have to try that!" Beth said excitedly.

"I can remember daddy laughing and saying when he showed me the trick saying "Don't go cheap on me now and try nickels. They don't work, because the edges are smooth!" Bessie May said with a broad winsome smile.

10

A Fox Builds A Chicken House

We need to quit talking about hunting and fishing and air guns and such and get down to some trading business. Marvis said stoppering the jug and putting it up for now.

"That's fine with us, we already made us a trade with your boys though." Slim said.

"Well, you traded for some fresh eggs but I hear you wanted some live chickens also." Marvis said watching the carefully.

"Well yes we did but we had more of an interest in some laying hens than eating ones. It just depends, we definitely are interested in some broiler chickens also." Steve said.

"You ever raised chickens before?" Marvis asked

"Yea when I was a boy, we fed them grain back then though and weren't totally free ranging like yours are. We always had an evening feeding of grain or other treat to lure the flock back to the chicken coop for roosting. When it was breeding time for the hawks, I feed the flock in the morning and let them out a little later. They're allowed to roam until they put themselves up to roost at night. Thing is I don't have any grain, you got any to sell?" Steve asked

"Nah I don't have any, I got something for you to use until you figure out different if want. Fodder is nothing more than soaking and sprouting seeds. It is so easy yet so cost effective. You can sprout many different kinds of seeds, but my personal favorite is wheat. I used to get a 50lb bag of wheat for around $8-$9 and still have a few but my chickens are doing fine without it. This will produce around 400lbs of food for your chickens. Start by soaking wheat seeds in a container for 12-24 hours. Then place them in a tub with holes drilled for drainage. Water the seeds daily and within 7 days you'll have you'll have chicken feed. Soak seeds daily so the fodder stays on a 7-day cycle. Fodder can be grown outdoors in warmer temps or indoors year-round. That would give you plenty of food to acclimate them to whatever kind of chicken yard your thinking of having. "Steve said.

"If you find yourself a push mower somewhere and decide to mow your grass, save the yard clippings and feed them to your chickens. You can also save and reuse the weeds from your vegetable garden and as chicken feed. Chickens are the perfect animals to stop wasting anything." Silvia said.

"Shoot you buy some of my chickens and all you need is a white bucket." Bessie May said laughing before explaining that she had trained her flock to come whenever she wanted them too.

"You see for well, I don't know how many years it's been now, it's been quite some time. You see I have always fed my flock from a white bucket. When I take garden or kitchen scraps out to them, I take them in the white bucket. From just a few weeks of age, they know that the white bucket means food. I do this to teach them to come to me and the yard for the white bucket. If they're out free ranging and I'm ready for them to come to the yard before roosting time, I go out with the white bucket. They will come running from every direction. I shake it a little to call any stragglers. They all come in to see what I've brought." Bessie Mae related.

"We can talk more about feeding them chickens later, could be you might just want to get all your eggs from us without raising any. How much do you all know about egg preservation?" Marvis asked and raised one eyebrow.

'You mean like how long they are good for without refrigeration or are you talking about something like a jar of pickled eggs?" Slim asked.

"I grew up on a farm so I know not to wash them unless I have too because you will take that preservative layer off and if you had to wash them because you had dirty eggs you use them first. Are you worried they will go bad before we can sell them in our Marina? Freshly laid eggs can be left out at room temperature for at least a month before your need to start thinking about moving them into the fridge. As long as you don't wash the "bloom" of the egg off your good to go." Steve said

The bloom is the natural coating or covering on the eggshell that seals the eggshell pores. The bloom helps to prevent bacteria from getting inside the shell and reduces moisture loss from the egg. In nature, the bloom dries and flakes off. Before they are sent to market, eggs are washed and sanitized, removing the bloom. About 10% of egg packers give eggs a light coating of edible mineral oil to restore the bloom.

" Do you know you can long-term storage them to last all winter? Chickens don't lay as much in the wintertime most places but we don't have to worry so much about that down here. Thing is during these spring months the hens are really producing and you got to do something with all them eggs to take advantage of this time period. Now I got a bazillion ways to preserve eggs but the two best are Lime water being a favorite in the 18th century and during the early 20th century, water glass was used with considerable success. We won't have any problem selling so called "Fresh Eggs" today that were laid 8 months ago and I bet you most folks won't know the difference" Marvis said

"I am not understanding you, are you saying you traded us for 8-month-old eggs?" Beth asked incredulously,

"No! Ha! Ha! We wouldn't do that to you darling unless you knew what you were getting. I know you all are full now but I am going to give you a dozen eggs I treated to take with you and you can decide for yourselves later or I can get Silvia to scramble up a few and you can have a spoonful to taste now. I suggest we do that because we got a lot of business to discuss." Bart said and when they agreed Silvia got a skillet out.

"I was never good at telling if an egg was good or not but I learned from my granny that used fresh eggs to make cakes with that you always bust your egg in a separate bowl first so you don't spoil your mix if its rotten." Beth said.

"That is good advice even with store bought ones sometimes. Now then let me tell you how to tell if an egg is good If you find a stray egg in the coop and aren't sure how old it is all you got to do is simply perform the fresh test." Bessie Mae said and then explained.

Egg Freshness Test

Sometimes it's hard to know if those eggs you've got on the counter or in the back of the refrigerator are still good to eat. The easiest way to find out is by using the age old and simple egg freshness water test. It's simple and it really works!

EGG FRESHNESS TEST

HOW TO TELL IF YOUR EGGS ARE STILL FRESH

1. FRESH
Place your egg in a bowl of water. If the egg sinks to the bottom and lies flat it is fresh.

2. LESS FRESH
If the egg touches the bottom but bobs upward it is still quite fresh.

3. OLD
If the egg is standing upright on one end it is getting old and should be used soon.

4. VERY OLD
If the egg floats to the surface it is very old.

This is a simple test and it works because as the egg ages the air space at the large end of the egg increases. The more buoyancy, the older the egg. Simply place your eggs in a bowl of water.

- A fresh egg will sink to the bottom and rest on its side.

- An old egg will float right to the top. When an egg is a few days old one end will tip upward at a slant

- As the egg gets older it will start to float to the top.

- Eggs that float to the surface are very old and *could* be spoiled although usually they are still fine to eat. The only way to determine if it is truly spoiled or not is to crack it open and check. Signs of a bad egg are obvious. If it has a strong smell or if the white has taken on a blue-green color, toss it out.

"Will your test work with them 8-month-old eggs your talking about? I still can't get over them being anything but spoiled after all that, you're not talking about one them thousand-year-old or whatever Chinese eggs, are you?" Steve said thinking of a very obscure Asian delicacy that looked horrible.

'No, I am not sure what one of them things taste like and don't want to know. I know they do it with clay and lime though. Lime water is what this batch was done with and no they don't taste like lime and these are about 5 months old." Marvis said as everyone got a taste of scrambled eggs that well tasted like and looked like scrambled eggs.

"That's amazing! So, what is the process?" Slim asked.

"It's very simple, basically its pickling lime and water and a little bit of salt." Marvis said studying them like he wanted to say more but wasn't ready.

"These come out of this crock right here." Beth said pointing tone sitting on the counter and everybody had a look.

"I hate to tell you all this but we sort of waylaid you out on the road and brought you here on purpose. Now don't get upset we ain't got nothing mean planned for you but it was important we talk to you first before somebody else had the chance to steal our idea maybe." Bart said solemnly.

"Yea don't be mad or nothing, you got a big feed and a piece of my nephew's birthday cake so no harm done if you don't like our business idea." Marvis said with a disarming smile.

"So, what's this business idea you had and why didn't you just tell us instead of going through all this?" Steve said warily.

"We had to watch you and get to know you first to see if we wanted to work with you. If you do decide to

work with us it's for good and we wouldn't take too kindly to anyone stealing our trade secrets or giving us the short end of the stick when it came to getting our fair share." Marvis said evenly but the veiled threat was there and even though Marvis was a kind gentle man you knew you didn't want to trifle with him and maybe his Iver Johnson semi auto 12-gauge shotgun by screwing him on a business deal in this apocalyptic world.

Steve sat back and considered what all that meant for the moment and said "Look you be fair with us we will be fair with you. I take it you have a bunch of them preserved eggs you want to sell and are needing a market for them am I wrong?" Steve asked.

"Bingo! You hit the nail on the head! The thing is we don't need that much toilet paper and the chickens are laying pretty much every day." Bart said chuckling.

"Well I don't see why you had to keep it that much of a big secret until now. We will be glad to help sell your eggs back at the Marina. That's what we actually wanted to do anyway!" Slim said.

"Well that kind of puts you in a tough spot now don't it seeing that you have more mailboxes to visit. They will have fresh eggs to sell and we want to sell off some of our surplus preserved eggs. Kind of puts us all on the hot seat you might say." Marvis said.

"I see your point but preserved storage eggs are something everybody can use and like you say they got a long shelf life to sit in a store over there and be ok for a while. Do any of the neighbors preserve there's also?" Steve asked.

"I am not sure if they do or they don't. Could be, but markets can get saturated as you know, take your toilet paper for example. I am offering you a steady supply of eggs that you can depend on and you are offering a steady supply of toilet paper which is a fair deal. If either one of runs out or saturates the market with either the price goes down normally. Now I could just trade you in bulk now for what we need because I am suspecting you got a lot more of that toilet paper put back somewhere but that kind of unbalances the market can't you see." Marvis replied.

"So maybe you want some kind of exclusivity arrangement? A non-circumvent maybe that we don't buy eggs from your neighbors so you can sell them toilet paper or something?" Slim asked speculating.

"Well something like that. I don't know how many folks would be buying eggs from you over at the marina and what kind of supply you might need. I should be able to supply everything you need but who knows? Also, what are you going to pay me with? Hat if I gave you 20 dozen preserved eggs right now on consignment and said bring me back my share of the money after you sell them at the marina? What should I charge?" Bart said.

"Now you got me on that, we had to find the product first to find out what we should charge and we were going to wholesale to the Ship chandler over there. I have no idea what retail would be. Keep in mind there ain't that much cash in circulation over there so think small in the pricing for what we ought to charge for cash." Steve said looking to Slim and Beth any indication they knew of a price to come up with.

"I don't think none of us have much of a use for cash if we can't get what we want with it anyway, ain't that right? Your town goods delivery service has a nice ring to it but the door to door way you are going about is too much work and too hard on the logistics of it all. I propose we centralize it, how about if that old general store you passed acts a pickup and delivery spot as well as a post office of some kind?" Marvis said saying that was his great grandfathers old place.

"Now I can see that working out just fine." Beth said considering that would give them a return address for these mailbox drops and Marvis could just hand them want lists as they came back and forth to town.

"We ain't done yet, see commerce has got to flow two ways here. We don't always want to be paid in toilet paper and you might get tired of getting paid in preserved eggs all the time. We want that place to be like a trading post and adjust our accounts in all kinds of goods and services. Might even make it the headquarters for a farmer's co-op of sorts. I don't know about that part, it requires further discussion." Bart said.

"Well I can't speak for everyone, we got lots of partners in this deal on our side by the way, but I think that could be worked out easily. We can swap you now for your personal needs paper goods wise and work out some kind of mutual consignments in the future. How does that sound?" Slim said.

"Sounds like, pardon the pun we are going to be getting a shit load of toilet paper but that's ok I am a Prepper!" Bart said sticking his hand out.

"So, the old country store is going to open its doors again and be the post office too? "Marvis said sticking his hand out also.

"I don't see why not!" Steve said and then said keep in mind their friends back at the beach might have some details they wanted ironed out before shaking the men's hands and Slim and Beth doing the same happily.

"Now then, we got another business proposal for you. We want you to build us an egg factory." Marvis said with a clever smile.

"An egg factory? What in the world is an egg factory and why ask us to build it?" Slim asked.

"Well the kind of egg factory I got in mind requires supplies, supplies we ain't got but you can get. You remember I told you about them two egg preservation methods?" Well we running short on supply's there and need some more ingredients." Marvis said with a grin.

"We can try to help you out but that pickling lime and that chemical you mentioned whatever it was ain't going to be easy to find. I take it no more preserved eggs when you run out of it?" Steve said pondering where to even look for such an odd commodity.

"Nah even if you can't find it I still have tons of other ways to preserve eggs. Hell, you can cover them up with wood ash to make them last longer also. You won't have no problem finding that pickling lime, I know where a bunch of it is and I got you a few other places to look for that sodium silicate that should have some sitting around. So, we got a deal then? You going to help us build our egg factory?" Marvis said.

"Why of course we will if you know where to get some and it is not too dangerous to go after. So you want us to supply the materials to preserve the eggs and you supply the eggs from your chickens? Or are talking about preserving your neighbors eggs also!" Slim said starting to catch on to the factory aspect of this egg preservation, trading post, post office thing that was materializing by the moment.

"Like you say, there are details to be ironed out but they are little ones. If the neighbors don't already know how to preserve eggs our way I kind of like to keep our secret sauce to ourselves. And if they do know how to do it which a lot might, it's a pretty common old-style way of doing it, we would still have a market for the chemicals and we could if we wanted to trade them for eggs. Also seeing that we are the drop off and delivery point for all these items we have a say in who gets what for what price." Marvis said pretty much creating a monopoly for him and Bart for the chicken and egg business for this part of the county.

"Why we are going to get rich if we can find those chemicals!" Beth said with a huge grin.

"Yes, we are!" Marvis said with a Kool Aid Pitcher man smile ear to ear.

"So how hard is it to get at these chemicals? You said you knew where a bunch was?" Slim asked.

"Shouldn't be hard at all to get what we need and we can help you if you get us some gas so we can come to town. We got several places to check for it, I doubt anyone carried it all off. Most dangerous one I reckon to acquire is sodium silicate which shouldn't be too hard to locate and worst-case scenario I can make it if we can find some lye and silica cat litter." Bart said.

(Back of book contains instructions for preserving eggs as well as making water glass!)

"You might be able to find some in the auto parts stores or Walmart for example. Water glass (sodium silicate) it is what shady used car dealers (back in the good ole days) put in the old clunkers to disguise failing radiators, leaking gaskets and weeping freeze plugs. When exposed to heat and air, the sodium silicate crystalizes and eventually plugs the leak. It's a sort of a lousy band-aid repair because it also crystalizes in the neck of the radiator and will probably cause more problems due to its corrosive nature. You can read the labels at the auto parts store on stuff like block dealer to see if it's in there. Pharmacy's sell it, Tractor supply sells it as cement floor sealer." Marvis said listing a few likely locations.

"We need to try to get some of them stoneware crocks somewhere if you can come up with any to do the egg waterglass or lime water thing, try antique stores, museums etc. to find them and since you down their trading put the word out your looking for some, no telling who might bring what to you. Regular big jars like mayonnaise etc. will work also." Bart said.

"We ought to be able to come up with that. I ain't to keen on going around any looted Walmart though. I suppose we could all go as an armed foraging group or something though to reduce our chances of running into any trouble. Where do you get that pickling lime stuff at?" Slim asked.

"They have calcium hydroxide or slack lime in building supply stores in 50lb bags. That will be the easiest thing to get to make lime water with and we would probably never run out of it. A gallon of water glass properly diluted and mixed should be enough to store about 60 to 70 dozen eggs. Its same thing as pickling lime." Marvis said.

"We should be able to have bags of that stuff the next trip! I will see about scaring you up some gas also to come help us on a few things also." Slim said getting excited

"I know for a fact that you are going to eat up those eggs you traded for pretty quick but if you ever want to do a short-term preservation trick I got one for you. Thermostabilization is the immersion of the egg for a short time in boiling water to coagulate a thin film of albumen immediately beneath the shell membrane. This method was rather extensively practiced by housewives of the late 19th century. Mild heating destroyed spoilage organisms but didn't cook the eggs. If you keep them in a cool place, thermostabilized eggs coated with oil will keep for several months, although some mold growth may take place." Silvia said.

"We are going to have us an egg factory!" Slim said with a broad grin and then suggested to Marvis that he uncork that jug again and pour them a round.

Pretty soon before sundown it was time to get on the road and get down to their fish camp for the night. They all said their hearty farewells and agreed to hook up the next day. Steve got in the big Cadillac and drove his wife and friend back to his house without incident and they got ready for night fall.

"Well I don't know about you but I have had myself more than one full day of surprises and adventures! Between all that food and keeping up with them boys and their parents wheeling and dealing, I am not going to be long for my bed tonight. Steve said sitting on the front porch back at the fish camp.

"I am dreading doing the mailbox run tomorrow and putting notes in those boxes to send their requests to Marvis's General Store. I sure hope we don't run into anyone. I am glad they are having their boys do half of them for us." Slim said.

"Me to and we got to get up and do it all again tomorrow! I feel like a yo-yo, we no sooner get here than we got to turn around and go back to the beach. Now I ain't going to be minding going by Bessie May and Marvis's house for baked chicken at one o'clock today in anyway though. I tell you, us running up on those families has turned into some kind of miracle! I just hope that Marvis keeps that jug of his put up, I only had three shots of the

"White Likker" and I swear I still feel tipsy." Beth said regarding the moonshine Marvis called stump knocker.

"Yea they seem like real nice folks, but I agree with you on that white lightening, I think I scalded my tongue and curled my toes! That stuff is made to keep you a half of a bubble off of level for a while I am, telling you!" Steve said chuckling having had quite a few more drinks with Slim and Bart than she did.

"I asked him did he have any more of it he would consider trading for, but unfortunately, he said no. He said he would fix that shortage once the trading post got up and running good though." Slim replied wishing he had some of that fire water to share with Travis.

"Bessie May said she was going to show me her wood stove today. She said Marvis moved it out of the old family cabin to their house after the grid went down. I always wanted to learn to cook on one of those things. When we are out hunting for those stoneware crocks we need to try and find us one." Beth said and then related that was how the woman had managed to make Stanley's birthday cake.

"Marvis said he would give me some tomato and squash seeds but the planting season was pretty much over for new plantings outside." Steve said.

"That's something else that we can sell and trade for." Slim said thinking it was just about too much to consider how their world had changed for the better in only one day.

"Lots of possibilities, are we going to load up now or wait and cram that car with more paper goods tomorrow?" Steve said.

"Might as well get it done now, it will give us some extra room in the cabin." Slim remarked.

The previous load of paper goods that Tina and Travis had dropped off after they had first found the restaurant supply trailer was stashed under bunks, in the middle of the floor and on top of the counters already. Getting rid of the majority of it to put in Marvis's store on account and finish their trade would get it out the way. They were to pick up their first shipment of 20 dozen eggs tomorrow and they were excited to hear the buzz of folks talking about them returning so quick with the goods to the marina tomorrow afternoon. That was going to be one bunch of happy people! Travis and Tina would probably be the happiest of them all because they had done more to conceive of and get this chicken and egg plan going than most. Things were looking up and the community could worry less about food and keep the reconstruction of society going now.

Back at the beach house the next day Travis and Tina peered out the glass patio door leading out to the backyard as the rain obscured their view of the dock and the branch off Grand Lagoon. "This sitting and waiting around for the weather to lift was hell" Travis had grumbled numerous times this morning. He and Tina had prepped for all kind of disaster contingencies but boredom was not one they had given much of a glance at except for a pack of playing cards in the bug out bag. Those cards unfortunately had been left back at the Fish camp and were not available here to do them any good.

Steve, Beth and Slim were supposed to carry them back to them in a day or two from there depending on how their mail box solicitations to trade with them had produced

Carl and Wilma were still in the living room snoozing. They had evidently decided to go back to bed this morning after finding out no one could come up with a miraculous way of heating up any coffee in the confines of the house and all the wood outside was wet even if they did get a break in the weather. Getting up at the crack of dawn was just something everyone did these days

"You know Tina, we are sort of a pair of odd beings now, we know a lot, we got some prepper stuff but we are getting outdated all the time and a bit old for this new adventure. I admit we are better equipped mentally than the younger ones in some ways but comparing ourselves to them boys and girls who grew up on the coast hunting and fishing we are babes in the woods. .

"You know what Frazier and Martha are doing? She is keeping a daily journal of their adventure and Frazier is writing a fiction book about it of all things! Of course, they are doing it long hand and writing in in spiral notebooks but they sit down and take the take time to do it. How about you do what Frazier said he and Martha does to adapting to aging in the apocalypse. He writes his fiction books for their entertainment and carries his preps based on what do I need now to get a task done and what will I always need just to survive with tool wise daily and doesn't worry about the rest. That's all pretty much any of us can do these days , young or old except that book writing part. I couldn't do that. I got to ask him if he has any of his paperbacks with him, I would like to read one." Tina said.

" Me too, I would love to get a look at that journal Martha keeps but Frazer said not just yet because it had notes on places they like to visit for scrounging stuff that might be valuable to them later and they just soon that information not become common knowledge." Travis replied.

"You know what you don't see in those prepper fiction and survival books? How dog tired you are going to be just walking the neighborhood to a squirrel tree to try your luck hunting! I tell you what, the daily push push grind of trying to find some food every day and look over your back every minute wore me out the first week we had to get serious about doing it and its been downhill ever sense. I sure hope this egg deal comes through to take some of the pressure of living off. I suppose the eggs will keep longer this winter if we kept them outside but how long will they stay good inside in this summer heat with no refrigeration.?" Tina said.

" Martha said a week or two was no problem so I am going with that. Do you think we will get lucky and Steve and them come back today?" Travis asked.

"Could be if they got lucky and found someone going down to the Fish Camp, otherwise they are going to be in hiding from the rain like we are today." Tina said.

"I don't know what we are going to have to eat today but I am going to call it "Hunters Soup" because I will always be hunting for something to put in it." Travis said and went back to looking out the window.

And please remember: Survival takes community.

All My Best,

Ron Foster

The subtitle of this book was an homage to the famous folklore story "Stone Soup"
Stone soup has many versions from all over the world it seems, here are a few for you to consider.

A Recipe for Stone Soup from 1808!

'Give me a piece of paper' (said the traveler) 'and I'll write it down for you,' which he did as follows: —A receipt to-make Stone Soup. 'Take a large stone, put it into a sufficient quantity of boiling water; properly season it with pepper and salt; add three or four pounds of good beef, a handful of pot-herbs, some onions, a cabbage, and three or four carrots. When the soup is made the stone may be thrown away.' Published in *The American magazine of wit, 1808*

In McGovern's version of Stone Soup, there is a young boy who is very hungry from his travels. He discovers a large house where an old lady is living and stops to ask if she has any food to spare. The old lady tells the boy that she has nothing she can give him to eat. The young boy then asks her for a stone and then a pot, and tells the old lady that he will make soup from a stone. The old lady is so curious, that she gets caught up in his directions for making stone soup and the boy tricks her into making a meal for him.

Stone Soup by Heather Forest, is an enlightening story about sharing and the effect it can have on others. When two weary travelers come into a wealthy village, all the inhabitants deny them a meal. The two travelers publicly declare that they will make soup from a stone. Out of curiosity, the villagers provide all the ingredients, one-by-one, to make the soup. After all the villagers have made their contributions and pronounce the soup delicious, they learn that the real "magic" behind this soup is sharing!

A Fox Builds A Chicken House

What you need to Make Lime Water:

Hydrated Lime (or Pickling Lime) (Calcium hydroxide (traditionally called slaked lime)
Stone Crock* (Food grade plastic bucket or non-corrosive container with lid or cover)
Fresh, Clean, dry, **unwashed** eggs (unwashed farm eggs, not commercial that have to be washed and treated for consumer purchase, by USDA law)

Directions for using Dry Lime:

Pour a layer of the lime in the bottom of a crock or other container. Lay the clean, unwashed eggs on this layer, then cover with more lime. Continue to layer until your container is full and completely covered with the lime. Place a lid on the container and keep in a moderately cool location. 50-55 degrees is ideal, but the temperature can very higher or lower by a few degrees. The pantry or basement is a good location.   Make sure to label with date the preserving started and mark your calendar, so you don't tend to forget, especially if the container is in an out of the way place that can be overlooked. **NOTE:** Though my photos do not show it, layer the eggs with the small end down, so the yolk remains in the center and the air sac at the large end. Continue to layer in this manner, covering each layer with the lime.

You can leave the eggs in the lime for 6-8 months,

however in old texts, it was reported that the eggs would keep 18 months to 2 years in this lime bed. In ancient China, and in fact today, the Hundred year eggs are made by embedding the eggs in a lime-clay slurry. This method was discovered purely by accident, when some eggs were found in a lime and clay deposit, and the eggs were still edible. I must say I have seen those *edible* eggs, and the dark green to black yolk is not too appealing, however in the Chinese culture they are a delicacy and quite revered. I'm just not so sure why anyone that came across those eggs even wanted to taste them, however if it was the difference between starvation and aesthetics, I should imagine eating those was the best option. But I digress, it is in their culture and that is to be respected. We won't keep the eggs for as long as the Chinese do, so no worries, the eggs should look as fresh as the day they were collected.

Directions for using Hydrated Lime Brine:

Mix water with the lime. The water should sit 24 hours before use to dissipate any chlorine or fluoride, or use filtered or bottled water. Well water is fine to use, but again you may wish to allow it to sit 24 hours, city water should sit 24 hours.

The common ratio of water to lime is 1 cup water (8 oz.) to 1 oz. Lime. You may need a kitchen scale for accurate measure of the lime. 1 oz. is about 6 teaspoons of the lime.

Mix the lime and water thoroughly with a wooden spoon. Carefully place the clean, unwashed eggs in the brine solution, until the container is full, or you can just add to this solution as you have the eggs to add, until the container is full. Label the container and place a lid on it. Periodically check to make sure the brine has not evaporated and left eggs exposed. The eggs need to be covered with the brine at all times. Mark your calendar to make sure you don't forget the eggs, especially if they are located in an out of the way place. Check at 6-8 months, and the eggs according to research have been known to keep in the brine for 18 months to 2 years.

Ready to use: When you are ready to use the eggs, remove just what you need and keep the remaining eggs covered, whether using the dry or liquid brine method.

Caution: If using a crock, do not use a vintage one. Though they were typically salt glazed inside and out, there is a good likelihood that there was lead content; that lead can leach out of the interior glaze. I would advise using modern made crocks that are made without any lead in the glaze or in the stoneware. Vintage crocks are great for display, however not the best choice for food preservation. Lead was used well into the 20th century, so I would be cautious and use a crock that was made after 1960 or 1970, when research proved that lead was detrimental and was no longer legal to use in glass, glazes or paints. Be very cautious of any made in foreign countries that may not adhere to our regulations in this country.

Waterglass (liquid sodium silicate) has several uses, one of them is for storing fresh eggs for extended periods of time. Here is a quote from Lehman's ad: "Preserve eggs for months with Waterglass. Mix one part Waterglass with ten parts cooled, boiled water and pour into a large, stone crock. Wipe off fresh eggs with a flannel cloth and place in solution (eggs should be covered with 2"). Cover crock and store in a cool, dry place. (From "The Boston Cooking School Cook Book" by Fannie Farmer, c. 1886) Waterglass (liquid sodium silicate) - One gallon bucket will preserve 50 dozen eggs. Non hazardous; fumeless. $21.95 Water glass was a prevalent method to preserve eggs until the early 20th century, in particular in rural areas, before electricity was widely available. Its use has fallen off, but you can still preserve eggs using I (You can buy much cheaper at pharmacy, as for Sodium silicate

Sodium silicate, also called waterglass is an interesting compound that is used in a variety of things. Water glass is a glue, a high heat cement or refractory, used to preserve eggs without refrigeration and as a sealer for concrete.

Warning, this involves using a caustic ingredient and heat so wear appropriate safety equipment, face shield, gloves and work in a well ventilated are

HOW TO MAKE SODIUM SILICATE - WATER GLASS By MaxPower1977

You will need the following:

200 grams Sodium Hydroxide - commonly known as lye, you need the pure form, some drain cleaners are made from this, soap makers also use it.

300 grams Silica Gel - Found in those little do not eat packs that come with electronics, also used as cat litter.

500 ml Water

Heat Source - butane burner, camp stove, etc.

Long Stir Stick

Stainless steel bowl or pot

Well ventilated work space

Here are the steps:

Add the lye to the water, this will generate lots of heat and fumes, do this in a well-ventilated area.

Once mixed add a little silica gel to the mixture, this will react and create more heat and fumes, stir to mix.

Keep adding a little of the silica gel at a time to the mixture until it is al combined. It is ok if the silica gel does not dissolve.

Heat the mixture over your heat source until it boils and keep stirring. If it starts over boiling, turn down the heat. Keep stirring and eventually it will become a clear thick syrup. If the silica gel has coloring in it, it may have a tint to it, which is perfectly ok.

Let cool and store. It can be diluted with water depending what your application is.

VISIT OUR eBAY STORE!

www.stores.ebay.com/outsidetheboxoutdoors

OUTSIDE THE BOX OUTDOORS
SURVIVAL KITS AND OUTDOOR GEAR

BILL PASCALE
WILLIAMPASCALE@COMCAST.NET

EBAY: OTBARCHITECTURE   WWW.SURVIVALISTGEAR.COM

UMAREX GAUNTLET

2252604

$ 320.99 **NEAR SILENT**

The Gauntlet's 3,000 psi air tank is easily filled using the built-in, standard Foster quick connect fitting. For extended shooting sessions, a simple pressure release key (included) allows the compact regulated tank to be unscrewed when pressure is low. It can be replaced with another, fully charged PCP tank for extended shooting periods, without the need to carry bulky HPA tanks or a hand pump. Its fully moderated design means the Gauntlet is incredibly quiet. Both stealthy backyard plinkers and serious hunters benefit from its ability to provide rapid, near-silent, full-power follow-up shots.

Product Details

Product Group: Air Rifles
Brand: Umarex

Caliber: .22 (5.5mm), .177 (4.5mm), .25 (6.35mm)
Ammo Type: Pellets
FPS w/Alloy Pellet: 1000 (.22), 1200 (.177), 1000 (.25)
Stock Material: Synthetic
Barrel Length: 28.5"
Overall Length: 46.75"

Accessory Rail: 11mm dovetail
Weight: 8.5 lbs
Capacity: 10, single shot option
Trigger: Adjustable, single stage
Air Flow: Regulated, non-adjustable
Mechanism: Pre-charged Pneumatic, bolt action
Warranty 3-year limited warranty

UMAREX FORGE

2251357

$ 161.99

Modern style meets classic feel when the innovative Nucleus Rail that makes scope mounting a breeze is merged with a wood stock. The Umarex Forge is sleek, modern, and classic all rolled into one attractive pellet rifle. Just one glance and you'll just have to have this modern break barrel.

SPECS

Product Group: Air Rifles
Brand: Umarex
Caliber: 0.177 (4.5 mm)
Ammo Type: Pellets
FPS w/Lead Pellet: 1050FPS
Barrel Length: 14.8"
Total Length (inches): 44.8"
Capacity: 1
Action: Break Barrel
Trigger Action: Adjustable Trigger
Trigger Pull (lbs): 5.6lbs
Length of Pull (inches): 14.6"

UMAREX NXG APX KIT

2251601

$ 75.00 $~~78.06~~

The Next Generation APX from Umarex USA is the genesis of modern youth air rifles. It redefines the standard of airguns designed for younger and small-framed shooters with a multitude of modern-day features that includes an automatic safety-a feature never before seen on a pneumatic rifle of this type.

The dual ammunition APX features a progressive stock design that's ergonomic, modern and impact resistant. Its grip is designed with a narrow curve that's comfortable for shooters with smaller hands creating better control and a safer shooting environment. Its multi-pump action and easy-load pellet ramp is easy to use for right or left-handed shooters and it deploys alloy projectiles up to a velocity of 800 feet per second at maximum air charge.

The adjustable rear sight and fiber optic front sight protected by its sleek muzzle brake allows you to quickly zero in on your intended target when shooting either pellets or steel BBs. Mounting a scope to the APX is easy with its integrated tactical-style scope mounting rail system-another first in youth air rifles that provides a positive lock down to keep a scope on zero. All of these features combine to make shooting the Umarex Next Generation APX a target-busting experience for shooters of many ages.

' First in its class with an Auto Safety!
' EZ-Load Pellet Ramp

' Strong, Impact Resistant Stock

' Integrated Rail for Easy Scope Mounting

IJ70020Y-18 20ga Youth

$180.00

- 20ga Youth single barrel shotgun
- Same as the IJ70020-18 with a 1 inch shorter stock
- Accepts up to a 3" shell
- 18" smooth bore barrel with fixed full choke

- Single Action
- Blade front sight
- Black chrome matte receiver and barrel
- Youth size walnut checkered stock and smooth forend
- Folds in half for easy transport and storage
- Sling swivels on the stock and the forend
- Single extractor to pull out the shell
- Functioning hammer
- Internal firing pin rest which keeps the hammer from resting on the firing pin when un-cocked
- Length of pull: 13"
- Overall length: 32.5"
- Weight unloaded: 4lbs. 12oz

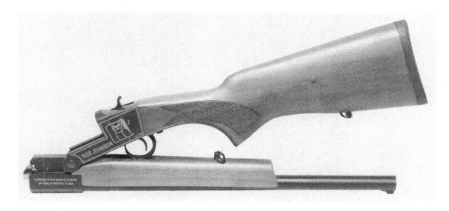

3-YEAR SHELF LIFE!*

*3-year shelf-life if stored at 80°F or less.

New, Innovative Product Option
- Provide your customer with a new food solution while backpacking, camping, hunting, hiking, fishing, and boating, as well as for home emergency preparedness.
- 3-year shelf-life if stored at 80° F or less; may be stored at 100° F for six months.
- Add variety to your camping food category.

9 Great Tasting Flavor Choices
- No water or heating is required. Just tear open and eat.
- Great cold or hot.
- Approved and used by the U.S. Military.

High in Protein and Carbohydrates
- On average, the meat-filled sandwiches and wraps provide 336 calories and 13 grams of protein per serving.

Compact
- 3.5-oz per sandwich
- 2.2 oz. per wrap

Inexpensive meal solution

For more information, visit bridgford.com/readytoeat
Toll-Free: (800) 527-2105, or email: info@bridgford.com

BRIDGFORD READY TO EAT SANDWICHES, WRAPS & PIZZA
Product & Nutritional Information

Product	Item Code	UPC Code 0-45700-	GTIN 1-00-47500-	Case Count & Weight	Tie-High	Case Cubic Ft	Case Gross Wt.	Case Net Wt.	Shelf Life (months)	Serving Size (g.)	Unit Size (oz.)	Calories	Total Fat (g)	Saturated Fat (g)	Trans Fat (g)	Cholesterol (mg)	Sodium (mg)	Carbohydrate (g)	Fiber (g)	Sugar (g)	Protein (g)	Vitamin A %DV	Vitamin C %DV	Calcium %DV	Iron %DV	Folic Acid (mcg)
French Toast	7145	01499-1	01499-8	8/2/3.5 oz	13x10	0.41	5.00	3.50	36	100	3.5	330	10	6	0	0	360	49	3	18	5	0	15	8	6	67
Cinnamon Bun	7146	01500-4	01500-1	8/2/3.5 oz	13x10	0.41	5.00	3.50	36	100	3.5	340	10	5	0	0	430	49	4	14	6	6	8	10	8	70
Italian Sausage with Sauce in bread	7151	01501-1	01501-8	8/2/3.5 oz	13x10	0.41	5.00	3.50	36	100	3.5	330	14	6	0	15	730	32	3	2	10	4	15	8	10	72
Beef with BBQ Sauce in bread	7152	01502-8	01502-5	8/2/3.5 oz	13x10	0.41	5.00	3.50	36	100	3.5	330	12	6	0	15	750	36	3	7	11	2	10	8	10	73
Apple Turnover	7158	01503-5	01503-2	8/2/3.5 oz	13x10	0.41	5.00	3.50	36	100	3.5	330	6	4.5	0	0	400	53	4	22	5	4	6	8	6	55
Sweet and Sour Chicken in bread	7159	01504-2	01504-9	8/2/3.5 oz	13x10	0.41	5.00	3.50	36	100	3.5	290	9	4	0	15	730	34	3	5	11	0	15	6	8	26
Pork w/ BBQ Sauce in flour tortilla	7571	01618-6	01618-3	8/2/2.2 oz	13x10	0.41	3.50	2.20	36	125	4.4	360	8	2.5	0	20	990	56	0	15	14	4	6	4	15	5
Mexican Style Beef in flour tortilla	7572	01619-3	01619-0	8/2/2.2 oz	13x10	0.41	3.75	2.40	36	125	4.4	370	9	3.5	0	30	1190	48	2	5	18	35	10	10	20	9
Pepperoni Pizza with Cheese & Sauce	7164	01750-31	01750-60	8/2/3.1 oz	13x10	0.41	4.50	3.10	36	88	3.1	290	12	5	0	15	850	29	3	2	10	8	15	18	8	23

Ingredient Statements

French Toast:
BREAD (ENRICHED BLEACHED FLOUR [WHEAT FLOUR, MALTED BARLEY FLOUR, NIACIN, IRON, THIAMINE MONONITRATE, RIBOFLAVIN, FOLIC ACID], WATER, PALM OIL, MAPLE FLAKES [SUGAR, VEGETABLE OIL (PALM OIL, PALM KERNEL OIL), WHEAT FLOUR, MALTODEXTRIN, CELLULOSE, MAPLE SUGAR, COCOA POWDER, GLUCOSE, NATURAL FLAVORS, EXTRACTIVES OF FOENUGREEK, SOY LECITHIN, CARAMEL COLOR, CINNAMON FLAKES [SUGAR, VEGETABLE OIL (PALM OIL, PALM KERNEL OIL), CINNAMON, SOY LECITHIN], GLYCEROL, YEAST, DOUGH CONDITIONERS [WHEAT FLOUR, MONOGLYCERIDES, DIACETYL TARTARIC ACID ESTERS OF MONO AND DIGLYCERIDES, SODIUM STEAROYL-LACTYLATE, ENZYME, SORBITAN MONOSTEARATE, CITRIC ACID, ASCORBIC ACID], SALT, GUM ARABIC, CALCIUM SULFATE, XANTHAN GUM, SORBIC ACID, BUTTER FLAVOR, TURMERIC EXTRACT), MAPLE FILLING (HIGH FRUCTOSE CORN SYRUP, WATER, DEXTROSE, IMITATION MAPLE SYRUP [CORN SYRUP, HIGH FRUCTOSE CORN SYRUP, WATER, CELLULOSE GUM, CARAMEL COLOR, SALT, SODIUM BENZOATE AND SORBIC ACID, ARTIFICIAL AND NATURAL FLAVORS, SODIUM PHOSPHATE], CORN SYRUP, GLYCEROL, TAPIOCA STARCH, CORN STARCH, MAPLE FLAVOR (NATURAL AND ARTIFICIAL), LOCUST BEAN GUM, XANTHAN GUM).
CONTAINS: WHEAT AND SOY.
CALORIES PER OUNCE: 94.

Cinnamon Bun:
BREAD (ENRICHED BLEACHED FLOUR [WHEAT FLOUR, MALTED BARLEY FLOUR, NIACIN, IRON, THIAMINE MONONITRATE, RIBOFLAVIN, FOLIC ACID], WATER, PALM OIL, GLYCEROL, CINNAMON FLAKES [SUGAR, VEGETABLE OIL (PALM OIL, PALM KERNEL OIL), CINNAMON, SOY LECITHIN], YEAST, SUGAR, DOUGH CONDITIONERS [WHEAT FLOUR, MONOGLYCERIDES, DIACETYL TARTARIC ACID ESTERS OF MONO AND DIGLYCERIDES, SODIUM STEAROYL-LACTYLATE, ENZYME, SORBITAN MONOSTEARATE, CITRIC ACID, ASCORBIC ACID], SALT, GUM ARABIC, CALCIUM SULFATE, XANTHAN GUM, SORBIC ACID, BUTTER FLAVOR, TURMERIC), CINNAMON FILLING (HIGH FRUCTOSE CORN SYRUP, WATER, DEXTROSE, CORN SYRUP, GLYCEROL, STARCH, CINNAMON/VANILLA FLAVOR [NATURAL AND ARTIFICIAL], LOCUST BEAN GUM, XANTHAN GUM).
CONTAINS: WHEAT AND SOY.
CALORIES PER OUNCE: 97.

Italian Sausage with Sauce in bread:
BREAD (ENRICHED BLEACHED FLOUR [WHEAT FLOUR, MALTED BARLEY FLOUR, NIACIN, IRON, THIAMINE MONONITRATE, RIBOFLAVIN, FOLIC ACID], WATER, PALM OIL, GLYCEROL, YEAST, DOUGH CONDITIONERS [WHEAT FLOUR, MONOGLYCERIDES, DIACETYL TARTARIC ACID ESTERS OF MONO- AND DIGLYCERIDES, SODIUM STEAROYL-LACTYLATE, ENZYME, SORBITAN MONOSTEARATE, CITRIC ACID, ASCORBIC ACID], SALT, GUM ARABIC, CALCIUM SULFATE, XANTHAN GUM, BUTTER FLAVOR, SORBIC ACID), ITALIAN SAUCE FILLING (ITALIAN SAUSAGE [PORK, SALT, SEASONINGS, DEXTROSE, MONOSODIUM GLUTAMATE, SODIUM NITRITE], TOMATO PASTE [TOMATOES, SALT, CITRIC ACID], TOMATOES, GLYCEROL, MOZZARELLA CHEESE POWDER [MOZZARELLA CHEESE PASTEURIZED MILK, CULTURES, SALT, ENZYMES], DISODIUM PHOSPHATE], SPICES AND FLAVORINGS, PARMESAN/ROMANO CHEESE [PASTEURIZED COW'S MILK, CULTURE, SALT, ENZYMES], OLIVE OIL, RICE SYRUP, SUGAR, SALT, CITRIC ACID).
CONTAINS: WHEAT AND MILK.
CALORIES PER OUNCE: 94.

Beef with BBQ Sauce in bread:
BREAD (ENRICHED BLEACHED FLOUR [WHEAT FLOUR, MALTED BARLEY FLOUR, NIACIN, IRON, THIAMINE MONONITRATE, RIBOFLAVIN, FOLIC ACID], WATER, PALM OIL, GLYCEROL, YEAST, DOUGH CONDITIONERS [WHEAT FLOUR, MONOGLYCERIDES, DIACETYL TARTARIC ACID ESTERS OF MONO- AND DIGLYCERIDES, SODIUM STEAROYL-LACTYLATE, ENZYME, SORBITAN MONOSTEARATE, CITRIC ACID, ASCORBIC ACID], SALT, GUM ARABIC, CALCIUM SULFATE, XANTHAN GUM, BUTTER FLAVOR, SORBIC ACID), BARBECUE BEEF (BEEF, TOMATO PASTE [TOMATOES, SALT, CITRIC ACID], BROWN SUGAR, MUSTARD, GLYCEROL, HONEY, MOLASSES, SPICES AND FLAVORINGS, BEEF BROTH, PARTIALLY HYDROGENATED SOYBEAN OIL, SALT, RICE SYRUP, VINEGAR, WORCESTERSHIRE SAUCE [VINEGAR, DEXTROSE, SALT, SUGAR, CARAMEL & ANNATTO COLOR, SPICES, FLAVORING, SPICE EXTRACTIVES], ONIONS, SMOKE FLAVORING, SODIUM PHOSPHATE).
CONTAINS: WHEAT.
CALORIES PER OUNCE: 94.

Apple Turnover:
BREAD (ENRICHED BLEACHED FLOUR [WHEAT FLOUR, MALTED BARLEY FLOUR, NIACIN, IRON, THIAMINE MONONITRATE, RIBOFLAVIN, FOLIC ACID], WATER, PALM OIL, CINNAMON FLAKES [SUGAR, VEGETABLE OIL (PALM OIL, PALM KERNEL OIL), CINNAMON, SOY LECITHIN], GLYCEROL, YEAST, DOUGH CONDITIONERS [WHEAT FLOUR, MONOGLYCERIDES, DIACETYL TARTARIC ACID ESTERS OF MONO- AND DIGLYCERIDES, SODIUM STEAROYL-LACTYLATE, ENZYME, SORBITAN MONOSTEARATE, CITRIC ACID, ASCORBIC ACID], SALT, GUM ARABIC, CALCIUM SULFATE, XANTHAN GUM, SORBIC ACID, BUTTER FLAVOR, TURMERIC), APPLE FILLING (HIGH FRUCTOSE CORN SYRUP, WATER, DRIED APPLES [APPLES, SUGAR, ASCORBIC ACID, CITRIC ACID], APPLE CONCENTRATE, DEXTROSE, GLYCEROL, STARCH, VANILLA FLAVOR [NATURAL AND ARTIFICIAL], LOCUST BEAN GUM, XANTHAN GUM, CINNAMON, APPLE FLAVORS).
CONTAINS: WHEAT AND SOY.
CALORIES PER OUNCE: 94.

Sweet and Sour Chicken in bread:
BREAD (ENRICHED BLEACHED FLOUR [WHEAT FLOUR, MALTED BARLEY FLOUR, NIACIN, IRON, THIAMINE MONONITRATE, RIBOFLAVIN, FOLIC ACID], WATER, PALM OIL, GLYCEROL, YEAST, DOUGH CONDITIONERS [WHEAT FLOUR, MONOGLYCERIDES, DIACETYL TARTARIC ACID ESTERS OF MONO- AND DIGLYCERIDES, SODIUM STEAROYL-LACTYLATE, ENZYME, SORBITAN MONOSTEARATE, CITRIC ACID, ASCORBIC ACID], SALT, GUM ARABIC, CALCIUM SULFATE, XANTHAN GUM, BUTTER FLAVOR, SORBIC ACID), SWEET & SOUR CHICKEN (CHICKEN, SUGAR, VINEGAR, WATER, PINEAPPLE, GLYCEROL, RICE SYRUP, ORANGE JUICE, BELL PEPPER, SOY SAUCE [WATER, WHEAT, SOY, SALT], CHOPPED ONIONS, CANOLA OIL, MODIFIED FOOD STARCH, SALT, SPICES AND FLAVORINGS, MOLASSES, SOY LECITHIN, CITRIC ACID).
CONTAINS: WHEAT AND SOY.
CALORIES PER OUNCE: 83.

Pork w/ BBQ Sauce in flour tortilla:
SEASONED PORK FILLING (PORK, BBQ SAUCE [HIGH FRUCTOSE CORN SYRUP, VINEGAR, TOMATO PASTE, MODIFIED FOOD STARCH, LESS THAN 2% OF SALT, PINEAPPLE JUICE, SMOKE FLAVOR, SPICES, CARAMEL, SODIUM BENZOATE, MOLASSES, CORN SYRUP, FLAVORS, SUGAR, TAMARIND, GLYCERIN, BBQ SEASONING [SUGAR, BROWN SUGAR, SALT, SPICES, PAPRIKA, MOLASSES POWDER, VINEGAR POWDER, MALTODEXTRIN, MODIFIED FOOD STARCH, APPLE CIDER VINEGAR], WORCESTERSHIRE SAUCE POWDER [VINEGAR, MOLASSES, CORN SYRUP SALT, CARAMEL COLOR, GARLIC, SUGAR, SPICES, TAMARIND, FLAVORS, FLAVORS, SMOKE FLAVOR, JALAPENO PEPPER POWDER], FLAVORS, SALT, SMOKE FLAVOR), FLOUR TORTILLA (ENRICHED BLEACHED WHEAT FLOUR [WHEAT FLOUR, NIACIN, REDUCED IRON, THIAMINE MONONITRATE, RIBOFLAVIN, FOLIC ACID], WATER, SHORTENING [INTERESTERIFIED AND HYDROGENATED SOYBEAN OIL], GLYCERIN, SALT, LESS THAN 2% OF: CORN STARCH, SODIUM BICARBONATE, SODIUM ALUMINUM SULFATE, MONO- AND DIGLYCERIDES, WHEAT FLOUR, GUAR GUM, SOYBEAN OIL, ENZYME, FUMARIC ACID, L-CYSTEINE, CALCIUM PROPIONATE, SORBIC ACID).
CONTAINS: WHEAT.
CALORIES PER OUNCE: 132.

Mexican Style Beef in flour tortilla:
SEASONED BEEF FILLING (BEEF, TOMATO PASTE [TOMATOES, SALT, CITRIC ACID], RICE SYRUP, GLYCERIN, RICE VINEGAR, SEASONINGS [CUMIN, CHILI POWDER, CAYENNE PEPPER, BLACK PEPPER, JALAPENO PEPPER], FLAVORINGS, SALT, VINEGAR POWDER), FLOUR TORTILLA (ENRICHED BLEACHED WHEAT FLOUR [WHEAT FLOUR, NIACIN, REDUCED IRON, THIAMINE MONONITRATE, RIBOFLAVIN, FOLIC ACID], WATER, SHORTENING [INTERESTERIFIED AND HYDROGENATED SOYBEAN OIL], GLYCERIN, SALT, LESS THAN 2% OF: CORN STARCH, SODIUM BICARBONATE, SODIUM ALUMINUM SULFATE, MONOCALCIUM PHOSPHATE, CALCIUM SULFATE, MONO- AND DIGLYCERIDES, WHEAT FLOUR, GUAR GUM, SOYBEAN OIL, ENZYME, FUMARIC ACID, L-CYSTEINE, CALCIUM PROPIONATE, SORBIC ACID), PASTEURIZED PROCESSED CHEESE PRODUCT (CHEDDAR CHEESE [CULTURED MILK, SALT, ENZYMES], WATER, SKIM MILK, GLYCERIN, SODIUM PHOSPHATE, WHEY, LACTIC ACID, SALT, XANTHAN, CARRAGEENAN, LOCUST BEAN GUM, SORBIC ACID, APOCAROTENAL [COLOR], ANNATTO AND PAPRIKA EXTRACT [COLOR], PRESERVATIVES [POTASSIUM SORBATE AND NATAMYCIN]).
CONTAINS: WHEAT AND MILK.
CALORIES PER OUNCE: 126.

Pepperoni Pizza with Cheese & Sauce:
CRUST (ENRICHED FLOUR [WHEAT FLOUR, NIACIN, IRON, THIAMINE MONONITRATE, RIBOFLAVIN, FOLIC ACID], WATER, YEAST, GLYCEROL, PALM OIL, DOUGH CONDITIONERS [SODIUM STEAROYL LACTYLATE, MONOGLYCERIDES, DIACETYL TARTARIC ACID ESTERS OF MONO AND DIGLYCERIDES, SORBITAN MONOSTEARATE, CITRIC ACID, ASCORBIC ACID], CALCIUM SULFATE, SALT, SUGAR, GUM ARABIC, XANTHAN GUM, GLUCONO-DELTA-LACTONE, SORBIC ACID), PASTEURIZED PROCESS MOZZARELLA CHEESE PRODUCT (CHEESE [MILK, CHEESE CULTURE, SALT, ENZYMES], WATER, GLYCEROL, CREAM, SKIM MILK, SALT, WHEY, SODIUM CITRATE, NATURAL FLAVOR, SODIUM PHOSPHATE, SODIUM/CARRAGEENAN/CAROB BEAN GUM, PRESERVATIVE [SORBIC ACID, POTASSIUM SORBATE AND/OR NATAMYCIN]), TOMATO SAUCE (TOMATO PASTE, CRUSHED TOMATOES, GLYCEROL, RICE SYRUP, OLIVE OIL, GARLIC POWDER, DRIED ONION, SALT, SPICES AND FLAVORINGS, CITRIC ACID), PEPPERONI (PORK, BEEF, SALT, WATER, DEXTROSE, PAPRIKA, SPICES AND FLAVORINGS, LACTIC ACID STARTER CULTURE, OLEORESIN OF PAPRIKA, SODIUM ERYTHORBATE, SODIUM NITRITE, BHA, BHT).
CONTAINS: WHEAT, MILK.
CALORIES PER OUNCE: 90.

For more information, visit bridgford.com/readytoeat
Toll-Free: (800) 527-2105, or email: info@bridgford.com

Black

True Timber-Kanati Camo

Viper Western Camo

Since 1959 the venerable AR-7 has been the choice of U.S. Air Force pilots who need a small-caliber rifle they can count on should they have to punch out over a remote area. Through the years the AR-7's reputation for portability, ease of operation and reliability has carried over to the civilian world. Today it's a favorite of bush pilots, backpackers and backcountry adventurers who, like their Air Force counterparts, need a rifle that's easy to carry yet has the accuracy to reliably take down small game.

Like the original Henry U.S. Survival Rifle, this innovative, semi-automatic model is lightweight (3.5 lbs.) and highly portable. At just 16.5″ long, when all the components are stowed, it easily fits into the cargo area of a plane, boat or in a backpack. It's chambered in .22 LR so you can carry a large quantity of ammunition without adding much weight to your gear.

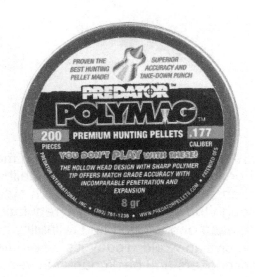

POLYMAG .177

This is the original Polymag polymer tipped pellet. Developed to offer unsurpassed accuracy and take down ability. This number one selling hunting pellet is perfect for all caliber air guns from .177 to .30 caliber. The hollow head body combined with the hard polymer tip creates tremendous trauma on your prey and creates an immediate take down.

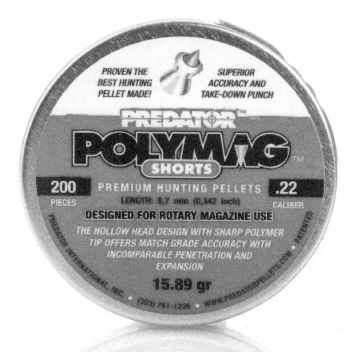

POLYMAG SHORT .22 CALIBER

The original Polymag was developed before the creation of rotary magazines. The length of the pellet was slightly longer than the majority of these magazines forcing loyal Polymag customers to load their pellets one at time into their magazine designed guns. The Polymag "Shorts" eliminates this need and offers air gunners with a magazine the same accuracy and take down ability as the original Polymags!

Made in the USA
Columbia, SC
18 July 2022

63645017R00117